BOOKED

BY KWAME ALEXANDER

Houghton Mifflin Harcourt
Boston   New York

www.hmhco.com

The text was set in Adobe Garamond Pro.

Library of Congress Cataloging-in-Publication Data is on file.

ISBN: 978-0-544-57098-6

Manufactured in the United States of America
DOC 10 9 8 7 6 5 4 3 2 1
4500582044

For Lynne, Stacey, Mary Ann, John, and Deborah,
some of the coolest librarians and teachers on the planet;
and to the best English teacher I never had:
Joanna Fox, the real dragonfly lady.

Gameplay

on the pitch, lightning faSt,
dribble, fake, then make a dash

player tries tO steal the ball
lift and step and make him fall

zip and zoom to find the spot
defense readies for the shot

Chip, then kick it in the air
take off like a Belgian hare

shoot it left, but watch it Curve
all he can do is observe

watch the ball bEnd in midflight
play this game faR into night.

1

Wake Up Call

After playing FIFA
online with Coby
till one thirty a.m.
last night,
you wake
this morning
to the sound
of Mom arguing
on the phone
with Dad.

2

Questions

Did you make up your bed?
Yeah. Can you put bananas in my pancakes, please?

Did you finish your homework?
Yeah. Can we play a quick game of Ping-Pong, Mom?

*And what about the reading. I didn't see you doing that
yesterday.*
Mom, Dad's not even here.

*Just because your father's away doesn't mean you can avoid
your chores.*
I barely have time for my *real* chores.

*Perhaps you should spend less time playing Xbox at all
hours of the night.*
Huh?

Oh, you think I didn't know?
I'm sick of reading his stupid words, Mom. I'm going to
high school next year and I shouldn't have to keep doing
this.

Why couldn't your dad

be a musician
like Jimmy Leon's dad
or own an oil company
like Coby's?
Better yet, why couldn't
he be a cool detective
driving
a sleek silver
convertible sports car
like Will Smith
in *Bad Boys*?
Instead, your dad's
a linguistics professor
with chronic verbomania*
as evidenced
by the fact
that he actually wrote
a dictionary
called *Weird and Wonderful Words*
with,
>   *get this,*
footnotes.

----
* **verbomania** [vurb-oh-mey-nee-uh] *noun: a crazed obsession for words.* Every
freakin' day I have to read his "dictionary," which has freakin' FOOTNOTES.
That's absurd to me. Kinda like ordering a glass of chocolate milk, then asking
for chocolate syrup on the side. Seriously, who does that? SMH!

In the elementary school spelling bee

when you intentionally
misspelled *heifer*,
he almost had a cow.

You're the only kid
on your block
at school
in THE. ENTIRE. FREAKIN'. WORLD.
who lives in a prison
of words.
He calls it *the pursuit of excellence.*
You call it *Shawshank.*
And even though your mother
forbids you to say it,
the truth is
you
HATE
words.

5

Giddy-up

she hollers,
SMASHING the ball
to the edge
of the right corner
of the table
with so much force,
it sends you diving
into the laundry stack,
trying and failing
to lob it back.

Loser does the dishes tonight.
You can't say that now, Mom. It's game point.

She drops a shot
right over the net
that you can't get to.
You're a one-trick pony, young boy.
Stick to soccer, she jokes, then
headlocks you,
hits you on the backside
with her paddle,
and soaks your forehead

in kisses
after beating you
for the fourth game
in a row.

Mom

used to race horses,
but now she only trains them.
Correction: she *used to*
train them,
which was pretty awesome,
especially when you
got to cowboy
around the neighborhood
or watch
the Preakness

from luxury box seats
with unlimited Coke and shrimp.
But she doesn't do it anymore
since there are no horses
in the city.
Last year,
she did get asked
to train
a horse named
Bite My Dust,
but when she revealed
that we'd have to move

to some small town
with no university
(or travel soccer team),
Dad said **No**
with a capital **N**.

Blackjack on the Way to School

With two sevens showing, you
say, Hit me! Coby curses
when you get a third. BLACKJACK!

Ms. Hardwick's Honors English class

is one boring
required read
after another.

So you've become a pro
at daydreaming
while pretend-listening.

11

The Beautiful Game

You're pumped.
The match is tied
at the end

of extra time.
Players gather
at center circle

for the coin toss.
You call tails
and win.

Real Madrid scores
the first goal.
Ours bounces

off the left post.
They make
the next two

in a row.
We make three.
They miss

their final two.
It's 3–3.
Your turn

to rev the engine,
turn on the jets.
Score, and you win.

Teammates
lock arms
for the final kick.

The crowd roars,
screams your name:

NICK HALL! NICK HALL! NICK HALL!

Like a greyhound
coursing game,
you take off

from twelve yards out,
winding
for the kill.

But right before

the winning kick
of your Barcelona debut,

Ms. Hardwick
streaks
across the field

in her heels and
purple polyester dress
yelling:

NICHOLAS HALL,
PAY
ATTENTION!

The thing about daydreaming

in class
is you forget
what was happening
just before ninety thousand fans
started **CHEERING** you
to victory.

So everything blurs
when your best friend whispers
from behind,

She's talking to you, bro,
and your teacher **SLAMS**
you with a question
that makes no sense:

The expression "to nip something in the bud"
is an example of what, Nicholas?

Uh, to nip it in the *butt*
is an example of
how to get slapped by a girl, you reply,
as confused
as a chameleon
in a bag
of gummy worms,

which sends
almost everyone
in class
into fits
of contagious snickering.

Everyone except
Ms. Hardwick.

Busted

Nicholas, I've warned you
about not paying attention
in my class.
This is your final warning.
Next time, it's down to the office.
Now, can anyone answer
the question correctly?

I can, I can, Ms. Hardwick, says Winnifred,
the teacher's pet (and a pain in the *class*).
What is the correct phrase, Winnifred?
Nip it in the bud, not butt, Ms. Hardwick, she answers,
then adds,
Sorta like when you prune a flower
in the budding stage, to keep it from growing.
Then she rolls her eyes. In your direction.

Precisely. It is a metaphor
for dealing with a problem
when it is still small
and before it grows
into something LARGER, Ms. Hardwick says,
looking dead at you.

Ironically, Nicholas, by not paying attention,
you have stumbled upon another literary device
called a malapropism.* Do you know what it means?
And of course you do, but before
you can tell her Winnifred raises
her hand and starts spelling it:
M-A-L-A-P-R-O-P-I-S-M, from
the French term mal à propos, *meaning*
when a person, or in this case, a boy,
uses a word that sounds like another
just to be funny.

Excellent, Winnifred, and since

you're such a comedian, Nicholas, Ms. Hardwick howls,
how about you finish reading
The Adventures of Huckleberry Finn
and find
an example of a malapropism
in the text
to present
in class next week.

ARRGGGHH!

----
* **malapropism** [mal-uh-prop-iz-uhm] *noun: the amusing and ludicrous misuse*
of a word, especially by confusion with one of a similar sound. Here's an example:
my English teacher, Ms. Hardwick, is a wolf in *cheap* clothing.

After School

Better pay attention,
or Ms. Hardwick's gonna
give you a good kick
in the grass,
Coby says
while you both wait
for Mom
to pick you up.
That was a malaprop, he jokes.
I know what it was!

Wanna play soccer? he asks.
Of course you do,
but you can't
because
it's Tuesday
and you have a ridiculous,
mind-numbing
two-hour special class
that your mom signed you up for
that you can't wait
to get to
because you get to spend
two hours

in the same room
with April.

Can't today, you lie.
Gotta catch up
on some homework.

At Miss Quattlebaum's School of Ballroom Dance & Etiquette

the boys
must address
the girls
as *Milady.*

> *Milady, may I take your coat?*
> *Milady, may I please have this dance?*
> *Milady, sorry my hands are clammy!*

After you learn
how to properly
shake hands,

> (*Firm, but gentle. Not limp,*
> *like a wet noodle. Up and down,*
> *for two to five seconds.*)

Quattlebaum chooses dance partners.
When she gets to you,
there are two girls left:

April, and a girl with chronic halitosis.
Guess who you get?
Yuck.

Chivalry

You plan to open the door for April
but the guy in front of you presses *PUSH TO OPEN.*

Still, she smiles your way, and you do the same, till
you see your mom out front, in the car, waiting

to embarrass you.
PLEASE. DON'T. BLOW. THE. HORN.

Hi, Nick.
Uh, hel . . . lo, uh, April

That was a fun class, wasn't it.
. . .

Sorry we didn't get to dance tonight.
Uh . . . yeah . . . I . . . uh.

Do you want my numb—
BEEEEEEEEEEP
BEEEEEEEEEP
BWONNNNNNNK!

Hi, I'm Nick's mom, nice to meet you, Mom screams out
the passenger window as you jump in.

Hi, Mrs. Hall.

Hello, darling, what's your—
Mom, stop. Bye, April. Please **Mom, drive.** ARGGH!

The Pact

Ninth grade is five months from now
when you and Coby have vowed
to have a girlfriend or die.

Ever since first grade

you and Coby
have been as tight
as a pair
of shin guards.
Star footballers and
always teammates, until now.

Even though
you're on the same
indoor soccer team
(which is cool),
for the first time ever,
you play for different
travel clubs
(which is not).

See, you both tried out
for the Under 15.
You made the **A** team.
He didn't.
But there was no freakin' way
the GREAT Coby
was playing
on a **B** team.
So his mom drove him

thirty miles to try out
for another club,
and now
the most dangerous player
on the rival soccer club
also happens to be
your best friend.

Best Friend

Coby Lee
is from Singapore. Sorta.
He was born there, like his dad, but

his mom's from Ghana,
which is where he learned *fútbol*
before they moved

here.
All before
Coby turned five.

You absolutely love soccer.
But Coby's married to it.
Committed like breathing

to it.
It's all he talks
and thinks about.

In math class
he made a pie chart
of the winningest

World Cup
jersey numbers
of the past fifty years.

Half of his room
is painted
red and gold

with cool posters
of the Ghana Black Stars.
The other half,

red and white
with posters of
the Singapore Lions

plastered
on the walls.
He's even got

a ball
autographed
by Essien

who he met
on his last trip
to Ghana.

Unfortunately,
you rarely see
any of this

because
your best friend's room
always smells

like skunk pee
and funky freakin'
feet.

Bragging Rights

After practice
you're psyched
to call Coby
and brag
about the awesome letter
your coach read
to the team,
wishing you could
see the look
on his face
when you drop
the news.

Instead, what drops
is *your* mouth
when he laughs
and says,
Yeah, we got one too.

The Letter

Dear Coach,

  Your team is invited to compete

in the Dr. Pepper Dallas Cup,

  the renowned world youth soccer tournament.

Since 1980, the Dallas Cup has given

  talented and up-and-coming players

the opportunity to compete against

  marquee teams from across the globe.

Notable alumni include David Beckham,

  Real Madrid's Chicharito, and the former NBA

  champion Hakeem Olajuwon.

Many top college and pro scouts will be in attendance,

  as well as more than 100,000 fans.

Congratulations on this honor, and

  we look forward to hosting you

this spring.

Dad's back in town

which means
you're in his study
surrounded by ten-foot walls
lined with books.

You're thinking
of April/Dallas/Anything
to avoid
reading

the last few dreadful pages
of this dreadful book.
On a large red leather couch
Dad lounges.

You're in a brick-hard
cushion-less seat.
Exercising. Your eyes.
Bored.

You sneak your phone out
while he's glued to
some book by a guy
named Rousseau,

who, ironically,
according to Wikipedia,
is quoted as having said,
I hate books.

Trash Talk

Nick, Dallas is gonna be insane, Coby texts.
On fire like butane, you respond.

My team's coming through like a freight train.
We're taking off like a jet plane.

Well, I've scored more goals than you.
Well, I'm on the better team.

We're undefeated.
So are we.

I'm co-captain of my team.
So am I.

*You know my ancestors invented soccer in China over four
thousand—*
You're from Singapore, dude.

Nick, I don't have time
to school you
on nineteenth-century migration
from Southern China.
The point is *I'm the quickest
striker*

in the league and
on earth.

IN YOUR MIND!

I'm the fastest bro
in the game.
Coby Lightning's my name.
In fact,
I'm so quick
I could probably
catch myself.

. . .

Nick, you still there?

PUT. THE. PHONE. AWAY, Nicholas

and finish your reading.
I'm finished, you lie.

What'd you think?
It was, uh, interesting.

Put the phone on my desk, and complete your assignment.
But, it's late, Dad, and I'm tired, and I have school
tomorrow.

Do me a favor and stop complaining about trying to be
excellent.
Whatever, you mumble.

What did you say?
Nothing. I need to use the bathroom.

Then go. And bring me a pillow from the guest room.
Why?

Because I need a pillow.
You're sleeping down here?

I am. Now, hurry up. We still have to go over our words.
Your words, you mumble on your way out.

Trouble

Coby
comes up
to you
at lunch
and asks
if you knew the twins
were back
at school.

Then
he asks
if you knew
one of 'em
was in the library
talking
to April.

Dean and Don Eggelston

are pit-bull mean
eighth grade tyrants
with beards.

They used to
play
soccer
with you

and Coby
till they got kicked
out of the league
for literally tackling

opponents
and then,
        get this,
biting them.

Fists of Fury

The twins live
down the block
from Langston Hughes
Middle School of the Arts,
which is why they get to go here,
since the only art
they're interested in
is pugilism,*
as evidenced by
the flaming-red boxing gloves
they sometimes sneak
into school
to punch
other kids with
(which is how they ended up
at the Alternative Behavior Center,
or the ABC, for the past year).

39

----
* **pugilism** [pyoo-juh-liz-uhm] *noun: the art of fighting with your fists; boxing.*
Like the time they boxed each other and Don ruptured Dean's eyeball, which is
why he wears a patch.

The library door

swings open
just as you and Coby arrive.
The twins grit hard.

Hey, PUNK, Don says,
emphasizing *punk,* pushing
you to the ground and

stepping on
your backpack.
They stare Coby down,

like they're gonna do something.
He stares back.
Don't let me catch you with my girl, Dean says

to you, laughing, then kicking your
bag again, before leaving,
and never saying a word to Coby,

because even though
Dean and Don are mean dogs,
always out for blood,

and prone to bite,
they only *bark*
at Coby.

When you walk inside

the library
April waves
from the back corner,
but before you can wave back,
Mr. MacDonald,
the librarian,
jumps in front of you,
holding
a hardcover book
in his colossal left hand,

a neon green bowling ball
in his right,
and sporting
a way-too-big 4XL tee
that reads:

Irony: The Opposite of Wrinkly

Welcome to the Dragonfly Café

Here fellas, take a book.
Uh, no thanks, Mr. MacDonald. We just came in to —

To join Nerds and Words? Excellent, Nick. We could use
some boys in our book club.
Maybe another time. I don't really do books.

It's a quick read—try it out this weekend.
Can't, Mr. Mac, we got a futsal* tournament.

A book brawl tournament?
Futsal.

Your foot's all permanent?
. . .

I heard about that thing in Ms. Hardwick's class. You
know I'm the king of malapropisms.
Uh, o-kay.

What's up with the bowling ball, Mr. Mac?
Big game this weekend too. Got to get my match-play
mojo on.

----
* **futsal** [foot-saul] *noun: indoor soccer played with five players on each side.*
We have our last futsal tournament this week, then travel soccer club revs up.

I don't even know what that means.
So, Coby, you want to join the book club?

Pass, Coby says, laughing. *Maybe if you changed the
name to Books and Babes I might join.*
Let us see what's in your dragonfly box and we'll join,
you say, before

The Mac starts,
          get this,
rapping:

Hey, DJ, Drop That Beat

The Mac drinks tea
in a dragonfly mug.
On the library floor
is a dragonfly rug.

The door is covered
with dragonfly pics,
'cause Skip to the Mac
is dragonfly sick.

Sometimes I wear
a dragonfly hat.
Got dragonfly this
and dragonfly that.

Around my room
are dragonfly clocks.
But please don't touch
my dragonfly box.

'Cause if you do
I might get cross.
Respect the Mac,
Dragonfly Boss!

45

Skip MacDonald

The Mac
is a corny-joke-cracking,
seven-foot
bowling fanatic
with a reddish mohawk
who wears funny T-shirts
and high-top Converse sneakers.
He used to be a rap producer,
but now
he only listens to

wack elevator music, because, he says,
hip-hop is dead.
When I ask him
who killed it,
he says: *Ringtones and objectification.*
Which is reason #1
why he left the music business
at age twenty-nine,
to become,
        get this,
a librarian?!
Reason #2 is
the brain surgery
he had
two years ago

that left him
with a scar
that runs across his head
from his left ear to his right.

But he's the coolest adult
in our school, and
to prove it, he's got
a Grammy Award
for best rap song
sitting right at checkout,
in plain view
for everyone to see
and touch.
Plus, he's won
Teacher of the Year
more times than Brazil
has won
the *World Cup*.
(And he's not even a teacher.)
So when he gets all geeked
about his nerdy book club
or breaks into some random rap
in the middle of a conversation,
most people smile or clap,
because we're all just happy
The Mac's still alive.

Huckleberry Finn-ished

Great discussion today, class.
I'm sure you all see why
Mark Twain is one
of our greatest literary
treasures, Ms. Hardwick says.

With only five minutes left in class,
it's probable she's forgotten
the assignment
she gave you,
which means
you're off the hook.

Tomorrow, we will begin
another classic
of children's literature.
One of my favorites,
Tuck Everlasting.

And your laughter gushes
like an open fire hydrant
'cause you could have sworn
You heard an *F*,
Instead of *T*.

I see our comedian is back.
Would you like to share
what's so funny
with the rest of the class?
Uh, no thanks, I'm good.

Winey, the know-it-all,
a.k.a. Winnifred,
the girl who beat you
in the elementary school spelling bee,
raises her hand:

Ms. Hardwick,
wasn't Nick supposed to
present a malapropism
to us today? she whines.
ARGGH!

Thank you, Winnifred,
Ms. Hardwick interrupts.
Nick, here's your chance to be funny.
Were you able to find
a malapropism

in Huckleberry Finn?
No, you say,

handing her
the assignment.
I actually found two.

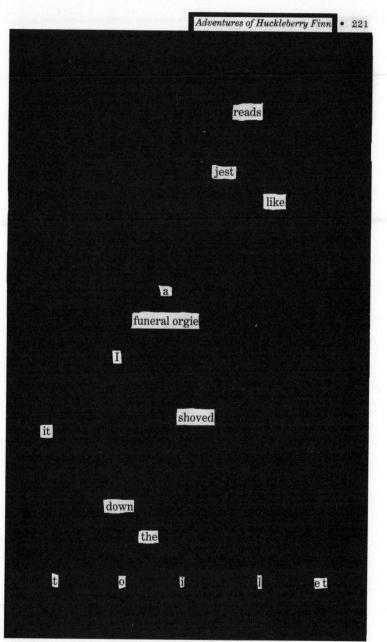

reads

jest

like

a

funeral orgie

I

shoved

it

down

the

t o i l e t

51

Class ends

when Ms. Hardwick
reads your assignment
then runs
into the hallway
cachinnating*
like she's about to pee
in her polyester.

----
* **cachinnate** [kak-uh-nayt] *verb: to laugh loudly.* In *Huck Finn,* Mark Twain misused the words "orgies" for "obsequies" (which means "ceremonies"), and "jest" for "just" (which means, uh, "just"). Get it? Yeah, me either, but Hardwick apparently did, 'cause we can still hear her *cachinnating,* so I guess my job's done. Nick Hall, SCORE!

Usually at dinner

Mom's asking
random questions
about girls and school,
Dad's talking
about some new,
weird word
he's found,
and you're eating
as fast as you can,
so you can finish
and get online
to play FIFA
with Coby.

But tonight is different.
the food's good, as usual—
fettucine alfredo with jumbo shrimp,
corn on the cob,
garlic bread sticks—
but,

      get this,
no one's saying a word.

It's like church
during prayer.
Dead silence. *Crickets*.
Something's not right.

Breaking the Silence

Can I have two hundred dollars to take to the Dallas
　　Cup? you ask.
That's absurd, Nicky, Mom answers.
Coby's dad is giving him five hundred.
It's not for a while. We'll discuss is later, she adds.
Dad doesn't say anything, which confirms
that something's up, 'cause he
ALWAYS. HAS. SOMETHING. TO. SAY.

Then it's all hush-hush again.

You clear the table,
Mom hugs you
longer than usual,
then you head upstairs
to cram
for your math test when
you hear Dad,
from the living room, say,

Nicholas, can you come in here for a minute?
Your mother and I need to talk with you,

and you pray
they didn't find out

about the lamp
you broke
while kicking
the ball
in your room.

No Heads-Up

When Mom says
she's decided to go back to work,
you're not too surprised,
'cause you know
how much she misses
being around horses
since Dad moved
the family
to the city
for his teaching job.

When she says
she's decided
to take a job
in Kentucky,
it jolts you,
'cause moving away
from your friends
and teammates
in the middle
of the school year
is vicious.

But when she says,
Nicky, your father and I

are separating,
it's like a bombshell
drops
right in the center
of your heart
and splatters
all across your life.

Thought

It does not take
a math genius
to understand that
when you subtract
a mother
from the equation
what remains
is negative.

Broken

After you finish
crying
and the sadness finds
a home
in what's left
of your heart,
you ask her
when she's leaving
you.

I'm not leaving
YOU, Nicky. I have to go
out next week,
meet with the racing team,
but I'll be back
every other weekend
until the Triple Crown,
and then I'm home
for the summer
and we'll figure out
how to fix all this.

How is she gonna
fix this shattered heart,
you wonder?

For the rest of the week

you can't sleep
your head aches
your stomach's a wreck
your soul's on fire
your parents are clueless
you fall asleep in class
you fail the math test
you're scared to talk to April
and you're trapped
in a cage of misery
with freedom
nowhere in sight.

If not for soccer,
what'd be the point?

Conversation Before the Match

You okay, bro?
Yeah, I'm fine.

It's okay to cry if you want. I heard it kills bacteria.
Nobody's crying.

Are they coming?
I think *she* is.

DUDE, parents suck.
Yep.

They tell you why?
Something about how they still love each other but they
don't like each other.

*That sounds like my parents, except they don't love each
other either.*
Yeah, well, they're screwing up my life.

So, who are you gonna live with?
She's moving to Kentucky.

What's in Kentucky?
The Horse.

So, what are you gonna do?
She says I'll be better off, for now, living with my Dad.

She's probably right. Do they even have soccer in Kentucky?
Dude, me and him alone is a nightmare.

But you can't leave in the middle of soccer season.
It's not like she even asked me to come with her.

Wait, if your mom's moving, who's gonna take us to school?
I don't wanna talk about it.

*Bro, don't tell me we gotta take the city bus. Why can't
your mom take us?*
Why can't your mom?   63

*You know she works early mornings. Plus her car is orange.
I'm not going out like that.*
Then we better get bus passes.

*Sorry your parents are splitting up, bro, but this really
sucks.*
I'm not trippin'. There's Coach, let's go.

Playing Soccer

is like
never hitting pause
on your favorite ninety-minute movie
but futsal is like
fast forward
for forty
supercharged minutes.

Game one
zips by
like a pronghorn antelope,
fast and furious,
and just when we wind
the corner to a record
thirteen-goal shutout

our goalie
goes down
with a,
        get this,
broken pinkie
toe.

Game two

is tied
with twenty-nine seconds left.

Coby passes
the ball

to you.
Their best player attacks,

steals the ball,
passes it down court

to an open man,
who shoots it

just left of our *sub* goalie,
who normally plays midfielder:

Buzzer.
Beater.

65

No Problemo

Coach says
we must win
our final game
to advance
to the next round
of the tournament.

We say, *No problem.*

When our opponents
run out on the hardwood
with their ponytails
and matching pink shirts and socks
carrying gym bags
        (probably filled with glittered smartphones)

We say, *No problem.*

Problemo

The girls
let down
their ponytails,
high-five
their coach,
then walk over
to shake
our sweaty palms
after beating us
five to three.

Conversation with Mom

How's your dinner?
It's okay.

It's your favorite.
Thanks.

*I heard from Ms. Hardwick. She said you fell asleep in
class. Twice.*
. . .

I know this is tough, Nicky, but you can't slack off.
I wasn't asleep. I was daydreaming.

Maybe soccer is taking too much of your time.
It's not.

. . .

. . .

I saw some of your teammates crying after the game.
They weren't even really crying. It was just mewling.*

----
* **mewling** [myool-eeng] *verb: to cry weakly; whimper.* I wasn't.

*Well, they shoulda been bawling, 'cause those girls beat y'all
like rented mules.*

. . .

They whooped y'all bad, she says, laughing and tickling.
Stop, Mom, it's not funny.

You're right, that beatdown was not funny at all.
They're ranked number one in the state. Nobody told us
that.

*Nobody should have to tell you to play hard. Your team just
gave up, Nicky.*
You mean like you and Dad . . . just gave up?

69

Dear Nick

*I'm sending out a search team
to look for your smile, 'cause it's
been missing. Hugs, April F.*

You Want to Talk About April, but Coby's Mind Is on the Dallas Cup.

Think she likes me?
Maybe we'll get to meet the Cowboys.

You think she likes Dean?
What's your hotel?

She said she likes my smile.
My cousin played in the Dallas Cup.

Your cousin Elvis, who drives an ice cream truck?
He played Major League Soccer for a year, though.

What should I do about April?
For starters, talk to her, dude. You've never even said hello.

I have said hello. Twice.
Enough yapping, it's getting dark. Let's go play soccer.

Can't. Gotta get home.
Why?

My mom's leaving after dinner.
The last supper.

Mm-hmm. Later.
Good luck.

Nothing Good About Bye

I'm sorry, honey.
I don't understand. Everything was going great. Y'all
didn't give me any heads up.

This doesn't change how much we still love you.
Mm-hmm.

How about a game of Ping-Pong?
Nah.

Look, Nicky, this is tough, I know, but we'll get through
this.
How?

I'll be back in two weeks, and your father and I will figure
some things out, okay?
Sure.

No cereal for dinner, and no skipping Etiquette.
Sure.

There are bus passes in the kitchen drawer.
Mm-hmm.

One-word answers now, that's all your mother gets?
Are we done yet? I have some homework to finish.

I'm gonna miss you, honey.
What about Dad? Aren't you gonna say goodbye to him?

We already said our goodbyes, Nicky. Now come give me a big hug.

. . .

The Way a Door Closes

From your window
you watch
love
and happiness
sink
like twins
in quicksand
when
she drives
away,
leaving you
suffocating
in sleeplessness,
out of breath
and hope.

Exhausted.
Trapped.
F
 A
  L
   L
    I
     N
      G.

The Next Day

In the middle
of Ms. Hardwick's
grammar lesson
on when to use *lay*
and when to use *lie*,
you lay your head
on the desk
and doze off. **ZZZ**zzzzz

In the hallway

after class
you see
The Mac
grinning
like he's just won
the lottery,
in a neon green T-shirt
that says:

Similes are like metaphors . . .

Check it out, he says, handing
you a sheet
of paper with,
     get this,
most of the words
blacked out.

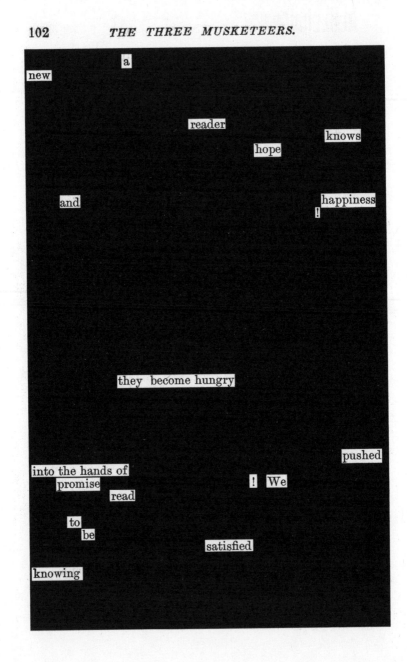

Conversation with The Mac

You inspired me, he says. *Pretty cool, huh?*
Uh, I guess.

Ms. Hardwick showed me your assignment. Magnificent!
It wasn't all that. I just didn't feel like writing three
paragraphs on why the book is ragabash.*

Didn't like it, huh? You're missing out. Huckleberry Finn
is a masterpiece, my friend.
More like a disaster piece. It was way too slow.

Hmm, you want a faster piece? I've got something—
Uh, I'm good, Mr. Mac.

I'm going to hook you up, Nick.
How about you hook me up with that dragonfly box?

You're still sweating this little old box? he asks, holding it
in his hand.
Why won't you tell us what's inside, Mr. Mac?

---

* **ragabash** [rag-a-bash] *noun: worthless, rubbish.* The book has a lot of bad
grammar, and my dad says it got banned when he was in school because it was
racist. So yeah, *ragabash.*

Mystery is good for the soul.
I won't tell anybody.

Maybe, he says, then nudges you out the library, before
you realize he's put a book in your hands.
ARGGH!

First Dinner Without Mom

Mustard mac-and-cheese
smells
as bad
as it sounds,
and tastes
even worse.

How was school?
Fine.

Did you finish the Rs?
. . .

He knows your pause means no.
*The good colleges look for extraordinary, Nicholas. You
need to know these words if you want to attend a good
college, Nicholas.*

College is not for, like, five years, Dad.
*Placement tests. Application essays. It's all words, son.
Know the words and you'll excel.*

None of my friends have to memorize a thousand words.
I'm not like you, Dad. Maybe I don't want to be extraordinary. Maybe I just want to be ordinary.

That's a load of codswallop. I give you the dictionary so
you'll know the world better, son. So you'll BE better.*

. . .

. . .

Your mother texted me today.

. . .

She misses you.
Do you miss her?

She's worried about you, Nicholas. Give her a call.
You didn't answer my question.

It's complicated. But we're both still here for you.
You're not BOTH here. That's the problem.

Let's just finish eating.
I'm done.

He tells you
to take the leftovers
for lunch.
Yeah, right.
After you trash them,

----
* **codswallop** [cod-swah-lup] *noun: something utterly senseless; nonsense.* I actually like this word, but not when he says it.

you clear the table
and make a
bacon, ham, and cheese
sandwich
for your *actual* lunch,
then head off to
not sleep
for the third night
in a row.

I'm sorry

Coby says,
juggling the ball
with his thighs
before passing it.

For what? You ask,
trapping it
with your chest.
For when we beat y'all in two weeks.

84

Not gonna happen, dude.
You kick the ball back to him.
I'm starving. Is your mom cooking?
Nah, but we got leftovers.

Watch this, Nick, he says,
then dribbles
to the center
of his backyard and

flame throws
a banana kick
so swift,
it basically splits

the air,
then sizzles
right into
his doghouse.

Hanging Out at Coby's

While he gets the grub
you check to see
if Dad has been
blowing up
your phone
with *come home* texts.
          (He hasn't.)
There are, however,
two texts
and three voicemails
from your mom
and it's probably not fair
that you haven't responded,
but hey,
life isn't fair.

She, of all people,
ought to know
that.

Conversation

Whatchu doing?
Just checking to see if the warden called.

Bro, you do know your dad's famous?
My dad blows.

I Googled him. Did you know he's got like nine thousand followers?
You're Googling my dad. That's weird.

I'm just saying, he's cool. Remember that time he took us to Fun Park?
Coby, we were, like, seven.

But we had fun, though. That Flying Circus ride was INSANE!
At least your dad doesn't make you read the dictionary.

It's hard for him to make me do anything, when I only see him once a year.
. . .

. . .

Your mom can cook, though. I love her food.

My mom blows.

Let's call April, he says

but when she answers
you can't think
of anything to say,
so you press
END CALL.

Man up, Nick.
Tell her that her smile sparkles
like a midnight star, or something.
Or give her these.
Then he reaches
in his top drawer

and hands you,
          get this,
milk chocolate
wrapped in shiny red and gold.
What am I supposed to do
with two bars of chocolate, Coby?

Not just any old chocolate, bro.
One hundred percent premium deluxe cocoa
made in Ghana!
So sweet, it'll give you a cavity
just thinking about it.

Home Alone

When you get home
you see Dad's note
that he's out
with friends,
which is odd
'cause you didn't know
he had any.

But it's cool,
'cause now
you can
fall asleep
watching
the Super Bowl
on ESPN Classic
without getting
a lecture
on the negative impact
of aggression
and violence
in your other
favorite sport.

Why You No Longer Play Football

Your first game
of Pop Warner
was electric.

In the fourth quarter,
a pass came
across the middle,

but before
you could catch it
and turn downfield

to score
the winning touchdown,
a brick wall

named Popeye Showalter
popped up
outta nowhere

and shut the lights off
for the longest three minutes
of your mom's life,

and that is why
you no longer play
football.

The next morning

you throw the covers off
lace your cleats
grab your burgundy
and blue headband
that matches
your Barcelona jersey
      (which you slept in)
throw your clothes
in the hamper
like he asked you to do

two days ago
and tiptoe
down the stairs
to sneak
out of the house
before he wakes up
and starts with
all the homework
questions.

The Homework Questions

Where are you going? he asks, sitting on the front
stoop.
Oh, hey, Dad, you say, startled. Uh, looks like the storm
missed us again. Gonna be a swell weekend, you say,
saluting the sun, wishing you had snuck out earlier and
avoided the *blah blah blah.*

So you're the weatherman now, huh? He asks, lacing his
running shoes.
You going running, Dad?

*Don't try to change the subject. Do you have a match
today?*
This afternoon.

So, where are you going?
To meet Coby at the park.

*Did you finish your homework? The **R**s?*
. . .

Average person knows about twelve thousand words.
Average president knows twice that, he says, *sounding like*

Morgan Freeman.

Even George Bush? you say with a smirk.

You want to go to Dallas, right?

I *am* going to Dallas. Y'all already said I could go.

You do what you need *to do, in order to do what you* want
to do. And I suspect that you still need *to do some reading.*
But, Dad, I shouldn't have to read on the weekend.
I have a game this afternoon, a game tomorrow, plus
there's three matches Coby and I are watching later on
TV, and I—

Read for an hour, then you can go, he shouts, already a
half block into his morning stride. *And don't forget to
call your mother.*
ARGGH!

Texts from Mom

My dear Nicky, I'm
assuming you've been eaten
by a black mamba

or pummeled to shreds
by a stampede of mammoth
shire sport horses

since you haven't returned a
single text of mine. Love, Mom

95

Texts to Mom

HAY, Mom, why'd you BALE?
Sorry I didn't call you
back. I've been feeling

a little HORSE. I
gotta TROT off. Soccer match
today. GIDDY-UP.

Jackpot

Miss Quattlebaum
finally pairs you
with April

for the waltz,
which is sensational,
and

one-two-three . . .
because
the right hand

must guide
the small of
Milady's back

two-two-three . . .
across the glossy hardwood
while the lucky left

three-two-three . . .
gets to hold
her hand,

twirl her out,
four-two-three . . .
spin her in,

pull her close,
nose to nose,
for the longest,

most awesome
six seconds ever,
during which

you quietly wish
that the German dancer
who invented

the waltz
had included
a kiss.

Insomnia

You make a sleep mask
out of one of your dad's ties.

You try counting sheep,
backwards.

You even pick up the book about Pelé
that The Mac made you take.

Nothing works.

So, you lie there,
staring at the ceiling,
remembering
those six seconds
with April
and the past six days
without
Mom.

Standing in the lunch line

Coby says, *Just ask your dad to take us to school. Dang!*
Trust me, you don't want that. He's got logorrhea,* you
answer.

That sounds disgusting.
It is.

Hey, Nick, there's April. Go for it.
Nah, I'm good.

Dean and Don aren't even around. Stop being scared.
I'm not. I just don't feel like it today.

HEY, APRIL, he screams, then ducks.
She turns and looks.
At me.

---
* **logorrhea** [log-uh-ree-uh] *noun: an excessive use of words.* If I had a million
dollars, I'd invest all of my money to cure this disease.

Big Trouble

You walk up to April, scared straight.
When's your next game? she asks.
You swallow

your gum and
string together a few
coherent words.

We, uh, play on, um,
Saturday
at the community center.

If you had more
than three dollars
in your pocket

maybe you could buy her
a cookie or an ice cream sandwich.
Instead, you stand there frozen.

I'm coming with Charlene and my cousin.
Score a goal for me, she says, then
shoots a smile

that sends you
to Jupiter
long enough

for Don
to "accidentally"
knock the tray

out of your hands
and bring you back
to earth.

Why'd you do that, Don? April snaps
as you pick up the food.
Nobody's talking to you, Ape.

Shut up, she fires back,
and gives him a shove
that only makes him laugh more,

and makes you
WANNA. SHUT. HIM. UP.

Stand Up

Her name's April, you say with a mean scowl.
How'd you like it if
I called you Daw instead of Don.

Daw? he says, laughing loud enough
to startle the few kids in the lunchroom who weren't
paying attention.
That doesn't even make sense.

Daw is the origin of your name, you continue.
It means simpleton, as in IDIOT.
He stops laughing.

As for your last name, *Eggleston,*
well, that comes from the Latin word
egesta, as in excrement, or dung.

So maybe we should call you Dumb Dung.
Now the whole lunchroom is cracking up,
April too.

Or better yet, how about **Stupid Crap**!
A guy in the back of the line hollers,
SHOTS FIRED!

Even the blond-haired cafeteria lady joins in on the fun:
Oh my, you just got cooked, son.
The place goes crazy.

It's like you're about to score
and everyone's chanting your name.
Nick Hall! **Nick Hall! NICK HALL!**

He charges, tries
to tackle you.
And then (What the—)

you snap
out of it and
realize

that none of this
happened.
ARGGH!

Back to Life

Say something, punk, one-eyed Dean says,
standing in front of you.
Wait, where'd he come from?

Stay away from April, he continues, *she's mine.*
I'm not yours, and you can't tell him to stay away from me,
April shouts back.
Let's go, Nick, she adds.

Dean knocks you into the fruit stand. You fall.
So do all the bananas and apples.
A hand reaches down to pick you up. *Let's bounce,*
Coby says.

This has nothing to do with you, *HALFrican,*
Don says to him, then daps one-eyed Dean, who adds,
Yeah, you BLasian, rice-eating—

But before he can finish
Coby covers up one eye, and hollers,
Yeah, well, I got my EYE on you, Dean,

and the place breaks out
in *OOOOH*s and *AAAAAH*s,
when all of a sudden, Dean

and Don both
bum-rush Coby,
who punches Don

in the stomach
before one-eyed Dean knocks him
to the ground.

You just,
        get this,
stand there, still frozen

with Bubble Yum stuck
in your throat and
King Chocolate

squished
in your pocket
while your best friend

tries to fight off
two pissed-off dogs
by himself.

Do-Over

You know
how sometimes
at night
when you can't sleep
and you're watching
the stars go
round and round
on the ceiling fan,
replaying
that one lousy incident
over and over
in your mind,

wishing
you'd done something
different
and that if you had a do-over
you definitely
woulda swooped down
on them jokers
like a vulture
instead of just circling above,
standing idly by
while your best friend
gets a black eye
and suspended
from school?

Consequences

The twins get
sent back
to ABC
for the rest
of the school year.

Coby gets
two days'
suspension.

You get
nothing.
Free as a bird.

The day after

the fight,
Principal Miller
sends a letter
to all parents
saying *racism*
will not be tolerated
at Langston Hughes.

Then we have
a *looonnnnng* assembly
and watch
Martin Luther King's
"I Have a Dream" speech,
which you know by heart
from listening to it
fifty-eleven times
at home.

Conversation

I got an email from Principal Miller.
Everyone got that.

I also got a call.
. . .

Racism is serious, Nicholas.
I know, Dad.

Were these boys picking on you?
It's nothing. I can handle it.

By fighting?
I wasn't fighting.

*Principal Miller says you were mixed up in all this. And
Coby got suspended? That's not good.*
They started it.

*Son, if they're bullying you, I can schedule a meeting with
their parents and the principal.*
Dad, no. You don't understand. I'll be fine. Can I get
back to my homework now?

The Last Time You Got into a Fight

There's only been
one fight.
It didn't go well.

Happened
in fourth grade,
during social studies.

Some kid named Travis
put his fingernail
in your hair.

You kicked
his desk.
He didn't like that.

Told you to meet him
after school
on the playground.

You'd been taking
tae kwon do lessons,
so he was in for a beatdown.

When you arrived,
he wasn't there, so you
practiced:

side punch,
knife hand block,
roundhouse kick.

But when he showed up
you were a little exhausted
from all the freakin' *practice,*

so as he rushed you,
instead of readying
for the easy takedown,

you called
TIME OUT,
and turned around

for a breather
when he jumped you
from behind,

and you never
went back
to tae kwon do.

Last night you couldn't watch TV

because Dad canceled
the cable,
so you missed
The Walking Dead.

This morning he tells you
that you're not getting
this week's allowance
'cause of your mountain of unwashed clothes.

And now Ms. Hardwick
is reading another boring book
in class, and April hasn't smiled
at you since the lunchroom brawl.

April is

Lovely
Intelligent
Magnetic
Electric
Red-hot
Easygoing
Nice
Courageous
Elegant

Caught

The intensity
on your face
is deafening, Nicholas Hall!

What? Huh?
If only you were concentrating as much
on The Watsons Go to Birmingham

as you were on that notebook of yours.
Care to show us what you've been working on?
It must be good, because your pencil's been

115

perpendicular for a good part of my class.
Come up here. And bring
your notebook with you.

The walk to her desk

feels like a death march.
Each classmate you pass is
eager and loaded,
ready to fire.

No other way to look at it.
Everyone's gonna know.
April's gonna know.
You're pretty much dead.

A bead of sweat drops
from your eyebrow.
Ms. Hardwick had to see it
hit her desk.

You hand her the notebook.
She glances at it, then shoots
a look that says,
You're going down, Hall!

Then She Smiles

If there were an award for worst teacher,
Ms. Hardwick would win hands down.
She's had a frown on her face
since the beginning of the school year.
So, when she smiles, you're flummoxed.*

*Well, it appears that
Nicholas here has been
doing a little bit of extra credit,* she says,
staring at your notebook.
Now you're really confused.

She hands you back your notebook.
*Nicholas, would you please share
this lovely new vocabulary word
you've discovered.*
She winks at you when she says *lovely*.

She's gonna embarrass you in front of everyone.
Do I have to, Ms. Hardwick?
It's such a wonderful, rhythmic word.
Spell it for the class, please.
You do, and then she goes in for the kill.

----
* **flummoxed** [fluhm-uhkst] *verb: to bewilder or confuse.* Why is Hardwick
smiling?

Do you know what it means, Nicholas?
No, you lie. (Why is she still smiling?)
Let's give Nicholas a round of applause.
Everyone does. Even April.
Class, your homework is to define limerence

and use it in a sentence.
Whew, you think, as you walk
back to your seat.
        (I survived!)
Ms. Hardwick isn't all that bad.

You escaped,
but just before
you sit down
Winnifred raises her hand
and starts
spraying bullets
everywhichaway.

Limerence

She says,
from the French word limier.
I can tell you what it means right now, Ms. Hardwick.
NOOOOOOOOOOOOOOOOOOOOOOOOOOOOOOOO!
Go right ahead, Winnifred.

Limerence is
the experience of being in love with someone,
commonly known as a crush,
but not any old crush.
A. Major. Crush.

119

NICHOLAS B. HALL
BELOVED SON. BEST FRIEND. SOCCER STAR.
2003–2016
DIED OF ONOMATOPHOBIA.*
MAY HE REST IN PEACE.

----
* **onomatophobia** [on-uh-maht-uh-foh-bee-uh] *noun: fear of hearing a certain word.* DEAD!!!!!

Coby's Back

When I was little,
my favorite toy
was a remote-control
helicopter.

I took it on vacation
one summer
and accidentally flew it
into the hotel pool.

I was afraid
to jump in
and get it
because I couldn't swim.

By the time
my dad got it out,
the engine had flooded
and it wouldn't fly anymore.

It was my favorite toy,
and I lost it.
I guess what I'm trying to say, Coby,
is I'm sorry.

I should have jumped in,
helped you in the fight.
He shrugs his shoulders,
tells you,

Don't worry about it, Nick.
Just have my back next time.
Did you get in trouble?
Yeah, I can't play in any games

for a week.
WHAT?! Can you still go to Dallas?
Of course.
Whew!

121

Sorry, Coby!
Yeah, just deal the cards.

Blackjack in the Library

*Let's play soccer after school,
Nick.* I can't. Got some chores to
do before my dad gets home.

You and Coby

sit on the floor
in the back
near the biographies,
playing cards,
whispering.

I already started packing for Dallas. You?
Think she knows?

Everyone knows, Nick.
How? Did April say something?

Nope, but Charlene gave me this note to give to you from April.
BLACKJACK.
SHHHHH! Let me see the note.

What note? whispers The Mac, surprising both of us.
I told you to be quiet, Coby.

Hey, why are we whispering? whispers The Mac.
'Cause we're in the library, Mr. Mac.

Not in the **dragonfly café. *WE DROP IT
LIKE IT'S HOT HERE!***

. . .

Fellas, let me ask you a question. Do you have a fave book?
Yeah, a checkbook, you say. Give me some cash.

Good one, Nick, Coby says, laughing along with you.
*Ha! Ha! I'm talking about a book that wows you. Just
totally rips your heart out of your chest and then brutally
stomps on it. That kind of book!*

Oh, WOW! you say.

When you find that kind of book, holla at us, Mr. Mac.

How was that soccer book I loaned you, Nick?
Uh, about that — it's a kids' book, Mr. Mac.

Yeah, but it's about Pelé, he says.
Really, it's a book about Pelé, the King of Fútbol? Coby
asks. *I would read that.*

You would?
Nah, probably not, but I'd definitely look at the pictures,
Coby says, and we both laugh.

*Okay, enough goofing off, fellas. And hide the note you slid
under your leg before Ms. Hardwick peeps it.*

Blackjack, Coby says as The Mac walks off.

Note from April

Dear Nick, Charlene and I think
"Limerence" is beautiful.
Meet me after my swim class.

Change of Plans

Coby, you still wanna play soccer?
Yeah!

Cool!
But I thought you had chores?

I can do them later.
You're suspect, bro!

Conversation After Soccer

Come on, man, just wait with me.
Can't, I gotta get home to watch my sister.

Just for a minute. I don't know what to say.
Just talk about the weather or something.

That's corny.
Nick, it ain't deep. Talk about what you know.

Soccer?

Yeah, talk to her about the Dallas Cup.

Good idea, but what if she thinks it's boring.
Then she's crazy, in which case you don't want her anyway.

True.
I gotta go.

But there she is. Over there on the sidewalk. What
should I do?
That's a shame.

What?

That you don't know what to say, given all the words in
your dad's dictionary.

Hey, where ya going? Come back!
BWAHAHAHAHAHA!

Conversation with April

Nice bike, Nick.
Thanks.

Thanks for coming.
Yeah.

Aren't you gonna ask me how was swimming class?
How was swimming class?

Well, Ms. Hardwick jumped in the pool.
What? No freakin' way!

Yeah, she wanted to test *the water. Get it? Test?*
That's funny.

Did you hear she isn't coming back next year?
Seriously?

Yep. She's going to another school. In Texas.
WOW! That's cool!

I like her.
Yeah, she's okay I guess, you lie.

. . .

Hey, I'm going to Texas.

That's nice. For what?
Dallas Cup. It's a pretty prestigious soccer tournament.

I like when you say words like that.
Prestigious? That's not really a big word or anything.

But you know a lot of big words?
Yeah, thanks to my dad, the verbomaniac, I have to read
his dictionary of weird words.

What letter are you on?
I just finished **Q** & **R**.

Wow! Like, what kind of words?
Like, uh, Quattlebaum.

Miss Quattlebaum?
Yep, her name is a portmanteau word, which means it's
made up of two different words. Her name is German.
Quattle means "fruit," and *baum* means "tree."

So she's Miss Fruit Tree.
Sure is, but we probably shouldn't call her that.

That's funny. What about my last name, Farrow?
Uh, I think it means "pretty" or something.*

. . .

So, do you like soccer?

Not really.
Oh!

Just kidding. I like watching you play.
. . .

Hey, I'm sorry about your parents.

Huh? I mean, what do you mean?

I saw what you posted about them ruining your life.
Oh, I wasn't, I mean, they—

My parents trip out too. It's so annoying.
I'm over it anyway.

Well that's good, 'cause I don't want you to lose your smile again.
. . .

----
* **farrow** [fair-oh] *noun: a litter of pigs.* No way was I telling her that she's a pig.

Here comes my mom. Raincheck on a big hug. See you in school, Nick.

Okay, uh, thanks, uh, bye, April.

The only thing

better than getting a hug
from April is the PROMISE
of getting a HUG from her.

Probability

If there are 278,000 people
in your city,
what are the odds
of you running
into the two people
you least
want to run
into?

Boy rides his bike

from the community center
to his home
like he's always done,
only this time,
before he even gets
a block away,
he meets trouble.

Where you going, Nick? asks Don, not
really caring about an answer.
*Yeah, didn't think you'd see us again
this year, did you?* says Dean.

The only thing
to do
right now
is gallop like a thoroughbred
as fast as your bike will possibly go,
and race
for your life.

Seems like to me, you owe us, says Dean.
For what? you manage to ask.
For getting us kicked out of school, punk.

. . .

Give us your bike.

Uh, I can't give it to you. I'll get in trouble.

Then I guess we'll kick the crap out of you.

Boy rides his bike
from the community center
to his home
like he's always done,
only this time,
before he even gets
a block away,
he meets trouble
and ends up

walking.

Kentucky

Maybe living there is not
such a bad thing. At least you
wouldn't be bullied anymore.

Breakdown

An hour later
you tiptoe
up the stairs,
try to sneak
past his room
before he—
     (Too late.)
Nicholas, come here.

*Very next time
you disobey me,
there'll be no Dallas.
Now do what you were supposed to do
and come home after school every day.
And give me your phone.*

It's not fair. IT'S JUST **NOT FAIR.**
You better lower your voice!

I HAD TO WALK ALL THE WAY HOME.
Where's your bus pass? Is your lip bleeding?

I rode my bike. I'm going to bed.
I asked you a question? And where's your bike?

They took it.
Who is they? And why'd you let them take it?

Why are you always blaming me?
No one's blaming you. I'm just asking—

I'm tired of this. You're always fussing
at me for not reading your stupid dictionary
or cleaning up my room.
You don't let me do ANYTHING.
You take my phone,
you took Mom,
and now you want to
take away
the last good thing
in my freakin' life:
SOCCER.

Calm down, Nicholas.
NO. I'm sick of it.
My life sucks.
I get bullied at school.
I get bullied at home.
I HATE MY LIFE!
I wish I was. Sometimes, I just wish I was—

What? You wish you were what?

Dead.

A Good Cry

The blasting rap music
in your headphones
makes you feel less sad
but still angry
about things, so
you start ripping
pages
from books
on your shelf
and only stop

when you get to
his dictionary, because
even though you're pissed
you're not stupid.
At the top
of the page
you almost ripped
is the word
*sweven.**

You fall asleep
repeating it

----
* **sweven** [sweh-vuhn] *noun: a dream or vision in your sleep.* This just may be
the coolest-sounding (*sweven*) word you've ever (*sweven*) read.

497 times
and dream that . . .

You sprained your ankle
on a dictionary while
moonwalking
with Michael Jackson.

Your parents
celebrate
their twentieth anniversary
at the Dallas Cup.

You beat up
Dean and Don
for picking on April, and then

you fall off
a mountain
but right before
you CRASH
you wake up
crying
in your mom's
arms.

What are you doing here?

Dad called, she says, wiping your tears. *I drove all night.*
We're both worried about you, Nicky.
I'm fine, Mom.

He told me what you said.
Mom, of course I'm not gonna kill myself. I was just
upset when I said that.

What about that stuff you posted online?
Seriously, Mom. I'm fine. I say stuff all the time that I
don't mean.

So, you lie?
C'mon, Mom.

. . .

. . .

Let's get out of here.
Huh?

Put on your clothes. Let's go to the field.
I don't feel like it.

That's a first! C'mon, I'm gonna give you a soccer
lesson today.
Do I have to?

Yes, but clean up this room first.
. . .

1 on 1

like lightning
you strike
fast and free
legs zoom
downfield
eyes fixed
on the checkered ball
on the goal
ten yards to go
can't nobody stop you

can't nobody cop you
till, like a siren in a storm,
she catches you
zips past you
strips the ball
trips you (fall)
watching her
dribble away
all the while thinking
it's bad that you got beat
by another girl
and worse
that the other girl is
your mother.

This morning

was just like old times:
cinnamon French toast,
Dutch pancakes,
Ping-Pong.
Now she's on
the pitch
talking trash
and you're feeling
a little better
until . . .

147

Conversation with Mom

I've been calling and calling.
Been a little busy with —

Sugar balls, Nicky! Too busy to return a call?
I'm not a kid anymore, Mom. I have a life.

Oh, you have a life, do you?
Yep.

Does your so-called life involve that little hot mama from dance class?
Huh?

Oh, really, you're going to play clueless.
No, she's just a friend.

What's her name?
April.

That's pretty. Aren't you too young to have a girlfriend?
I don't have a girlfriend. Plus, I'm almost thirteen.

You're still my Little Nicky.
Whatever, Mom. Let's finish playing.

Yeah, you can use the practice.

I'm good, actually. I scored two goals in my last game.

You'd know that if you were here.

I heard that.

. . .

Are you giving your father a hard time?

He's a jerk.

Be careful—he's your father. And since when is making you do your chores being a jerk?

So you two are talking again?

Nicky, he's doing what he thinks is best for you.

Making me read the dictionary is best for him, not me.

Your father loves you and he's—

Blah blah blah.

Don't make me hurt you, boy.

Can we just play, please?

So we're okay?

Yeah, as long as you stop tripping me. That's the only way you scored.

You're the one trippin'. That was no foul.

Maybe not when you played in the olden times.

If only your defense was as good as your jokes.

How long are you staying?

A few days, but I'll be back in two weeks.

You should come to my game this weekend. We're playing in New York, against the number one ranked team
in the country.

About that, Nick.

It's only New York, Mom. We have a ton of chaperones.

I'm afraid you won't be going to New York with the team.

You're gonna drive me?

*Your father and I have decided you won't be playing this
weekend. I'm sorry.*

WHAT?! YOU CAN'T DO THAT!

And Just Like That, Things Are Out of Control Again

You try everything. Coach
even calls Mom to beg her.
But, again, you have no rights.

Dressed in camouflage sneaks

and an army green long sleeved

FREADOM tee,
The Mac sees you
walk in the library
and hollers
      (right in front of
      everyfreakinbody):

IF YOU'RE LOOKING FOR APRIL FARROW,
    YOU'RE OUT OF LUCK.
NO BOOK CLUB TODAY, PELÉ.

Then he winks at you, laughs,
goes back to shelving books
and eating his sandwich.

Conversation with The Mac

Cowboys fan? he asks, sneaking up while you're on the
computer. *I saw you Googling Dallas.*
I'm going to the Dr. Pepper Dallas Cup. My soccer team
got invited to play.

This weekend?
In three weeks. This weekend blows.

The weekend's not even here yet. Think positive.
I had a soccer tournament in New York, but my parents
said I can't go.

Sorry to hear that, Pelé.
Why do parents suck?

Try a different word.
My bad, Mr. Mac. Why do **GUARDIANS** suck!

*Ha! Ha! Who your parents are now is not who they were or
who they will be. You may not like them now, but you will.*
Doubt it!

You get one chance to love, to be loved, Nick. If you're

lucky, maybe two.

It's just hard to love someone who cancels the cable right before the *Walking Dead* marathon.

Shrink

Instead of
playing soccer
in the Big Apple,
today
you're sitting
in the Center for Relational Recovery
on a pleather couch
between Mom and Dad,
staring at a quote by
a man named Freud
on the wall
behind a,
> *get this,*
psychologist
with a black and white beard longer
than *Santa Claus's,*
a red pencil in his mouth,
and a tendency to ask stupid questions:
> *What else besides soccer makes you happy?*
> *How do you feel when you're sad?*
> *Do you miss your mom?*
All because your bike
got stolen
and you lost
your cool

one night
and then
posted
that you needed
someone
to intervene
between you
and the monsters
and your cousin Julie
told your aunt
who called your dad
who texted Mom
who drove all night
and scheduled
an appointment
with St. Nick
who thinks your post
was a cry for help
when actually
you were just listening
to Eminem
and thought
the song was
kinda nice.

You miss

cinnamon French toast with blueberry preserves
homemade lunches
her headlocks and sloppy kisses
her saying *sugar balls* when she's pissed
her cheering at matches
Ping-Pong late Saturday nights
clean clothes on Sunday
double fudge milkshakes after church
dinner with real plates and glasses
her bad horse jokes at the table
both of them holding hands watching TV
family meetings
and, yes,
you even miss the group hug after family meetings
but, no,
neither your mom nor dad
is a monster
and you don't need
an interventionist.

When Mom Starts Crying, Dad Takes Her Out, Leaving You Alone with the Shrink

Camouflaging your fears doesn't make them go away,
Nicholas.
I'm afraid, okay. Now what?!

Now we try to figure out what to do.
I know what to do. I need to learn how to fight.

You think you need to learn how to fight?
Why are you repeating everything?

There are ways to deal with bullies.
Like what?

What do you think are some of the ways?
I guess if I knew that I wouldn't be here.

Why don't you think about some ways to deal, and when
you come back for the next session, we can—
Wait, I'm coming back?

Doctor *Fraud*

We have five more minutes
remaining, Nicholas.
Is there anything
you'd like to say
to your parents?

Other than
it kinda blows
that I'm here
instead of playing
in the soccer tournament,
I'm good.

. . .

Really, I'm fine.
The twins aren't coming back
to school this year,
and I didn't really mean
I wanted to be dead.
I just . . . I just think . . . I guess
I was mad, and if
they don't love each other
anymore, then
they shouldn't be together.

You only get one chance
to love,
to be loved.
And they lost theirs.
I get it.

Of course we still love each other, Dad says.
We just can't be together, Mom adds.

Let's explore that, says Dr. Santa. *What do you think*
about what your parents are saying, Nicholas?

I think being an adult
must be confusing
as hell.
Also, I'm starving.
Are we done?

Chimichangas

The silence
at dinner
is only interrupted
by the chomping
of chips and salsa
at what used to be
our favorite family
restaurant.

How Did We Get Here?

On second thought,
there *is* something
you'd like to ask
your parents.

According to a brochure
in Dr. Fraud's office,
adultery is the leading cause
of divorce among Americans.

Principal Miller would agree.
His wife got caught kissing
a man who wasn't Principal Miller.
Splitsville.

Your Uncle Jerry quit his job
and your Aunt Janice found out
when her brand-new Lexus got
repossessed. Separated.

Coby's dad and mom
never got divorced
because they were never
married.

But you still don't know
what happened.
So right after
the first bite of enchilada

you say: Dad, did you cheat
on Mom or something?
Beads of sweat cling to his bald head.
Mom stops chewing and gulps.

But before either can answer,
guess who walks up
in a T-shirt that says:
I Like Big BOOKS and I Cannot Lie?   163

Introductions

Mom and Dad,
this is Mr. MacDonald,
our librarian.

Dad stands up,
shakes his hand, and
The Mac, in,

　　　　get this,
red, white, and blue
bowling shoes,

kisses Mom's hand.
Dad kinda frowns.
Nice to meet you two, finally.

Sorry for the sweaty palms.
Happens after bowling.
Mom slips her hand in her lap (where her napkin is).

Your son talks
about you all the time.
I hope nice things, Mom says.

Actually, he kinda wants
you to take it easy on him.
Life ain't been no crystal stair

for young Nicholas here, he adds.
The silence is thick
and super uncomfortable.

I'm just kidding, The Mac says,
and then
breaks out into

a way-too-loud chuckle.
Well, I should get back
to my lady friend. Just

wanted to say hello.
Nick, they're a lot cooler
than you said, he pretend-whispers to you.

Well, it's our pleasure,
Mr. MacDonald, Mom says.
Oh, one more thing, Nick.

Did you finish that Pelé book yet?
You lie and say yeah,
'cause the last thing

you need is he and Dad
ganging up on you
over a book

that's never
gonna get read.
He turns to leave, and

your mouth hits
the table
when you see

The Mac's *lady friend*
in red heels
waving

from across
the room is
Ms. Hardwick.

Yuck.

Alarm Clock

Mom, I overslept, can you
drive me to school, please? It's
too late to take the bus. *Sure.*

Cool?

How'd you get to school?
My mom.

She's back?
She was. But she's gone again.

Why didn't you call me?
I overslept.

Dude, you never oversleep.
I just wanted to see my mom a little longer.

Yeah, whatever.
You want to come over after school?

Don't you have practice tonight?
We're just running today. Coach says we're ready.

Ready to get demolished like an old apartment building?
We'll see.

You see what April has on today? Whoa! Be bold, Nick!
Yeah, I should.

Be bold or go home.
I'm gonna do it. I'm gonna wear cool today.

Huh?
No more corduroys and turtlenecks for Nick Hall.

What are you talking about, Nick?
At lunch, I'm asking April to be my girlfriend.

Yeah, right!
Seriously, I am.

What are you gonna say?
Uh, will you be my girlfriend?

169

That's corny. Be cool with it.
How would you know? You've never done this before.

You either.
My dad gave my mom flowers once.

You gonna give her flowers?
I could, there's some yellow ones in the library.

Those are fake, bro.
Oh! Yeah, you right. Maybe I'm rushing it. She may not
even like me.

Didn't she already tell you SHE LIKES YOU?
I'm just saying, maybe she doesn't like me anymore.

Don't chicken out.
I almost forgot, we have a sub today.

Where's Hardwick?
All the English teachers are in a meeting today.

Cool, we can play blackjack.
DANG!

What?

I forgot to brush my teeth today.

So.
I can't talk to April today, like this.

I got some gum in my locker.
I'll just wait.

What happened to no more corduroys, chicken?
I'll wear jeans on Monday.

Brawkk-AWK! CLUCK CLUCK!

Not Cool

At lunch she walks by, smiles. *HEY,*
APRIL, Coby yells. *NICK HAS*
SOMETHING HE WANTS TO TELL YOU!

Bad

Don't know if it's
the fish nuggets
you ate,
Charlene's perfume,
the egg sandwich
someone's eating behind you,
or Coby's leftovers.

Whatever it is
sends you
running
out of the cafeteria
just as the volcano
of butterflies
in your belly

ERUPTS.

After Soccer Practice

Go wash up. I ordered pizza for dinner.
Nah.

Pineapple pepperoni.
Ugh.

You've already eaten?
Got a stomachache.

Drink some ginger ale. That'll help.
It just hurts. I need to lie down.

Are you in pain?
A little.

Come here, let me check your forehead.
Really? C'mon, Dad, I'm not a baby.

You're hot, Nick.
I just practiced for two hours, Dad. Course I'm hot.
Good night.

Maybe you ate something bad today.
Cafeteria food is always bad. We had fish nuggets.
Pretty nasty.

I'm gonna run out and get some activated charcoal.
Charcoal? Like for the grill?

Go get in bed, Nick.
G'night.

If you're sick, you probably shouldn't play tomorrow.
Oh, I'm playing in the match tomorrow.

Nicholas—
Dad, I'll be fine.

174   *We'll see.*

         . . .

You wake up at four a.m.

hungry, so you eat. Chips. Coke.
Thank goodness that's over. Bored,
you even read the Pelé book.

The Big Match

You and Coby
are on teams
that like each other
as much as crocs
and Kenyan wildebeests.

There's always
a skirmish
during
the matchup.

There's no beef
between you and Coby,
but you WILL go hard,
come with your A game,

'cause while winning
is wicked,
bragging about winning
is icing

on the steak.

Game On

You good, Nick? Coby asks
at midfield
for the coin flip.

Good enough to beat
your sorry team, you answer.
Not gonna happen!

Pernell,
your co-captain,
jogs up.

Coby daps you,
then goes to shake
Pernell's hand,

but Pernell leaves
Coby hangin'.
      (Told you it was a rivalry.)

Call it, the ref says,
then tosses the quarter.
Coby calls tails.

He loses.
You choose the ball.
Before Coby turns

to leave,
Pernell chides,
Sorry about that, chopstick,

then laughs,
but Coby laughs back,
then winks at him,

and Pernell is flummoxed
or pissed
or both.

Both teams take their positions.
You know Coby's smile
is misleading.

He's ready to pounce.

Score

You pass to the forward, whose
shot stings like wasabi, then
disappears into net. BOO-YAH!

Right before halftime

with the score 2–1,
Coby dribbles the ball
past two of our defenders,
speeds down the sidelines
like a cheetah,
then slants
toward the middle.
Pernell is the only
player from our team
left between him

and our goalie.
It's the matchup
you know
Coby has been itching for
since the start whistle.
As soon as Pernell charges
Coby cuts back
and you know
what's coming next.
Pernell dives in
for the take . . .
Oh, WOW!
Coby nutmegs* him.

----
* **nutmeg** [nuht-meg] *noun: a soccer trick in which the ball is dribbled between the defender's legs.* Imagine a ball of sun sneaking through the clouds. Lionel Messi is so good he could probably *nutmeg a mermaid*. Now that's hot.

He demoralizes Pernell.
Drops him
to his butt.
Treats him
like a dog.
Sit. Stay.

The crowd goes wild.
Both sides.
And when he ties
the game,
even you grin
at your best friend's
genius.

Payback is a beast, isn't it!

Guess Who's Back?

The Mac
in electric blue Chuck Taylors
runs over to your bench
during the break.

Hey, Nick, you didn't tell me Coby was a bus driver.
Huh?

He took that fool to school!
You want to agree loudly, but *that fool* is your teammate,
so you just kinda nod.

You don't look so swell, partner.
Uh, it's just hot out here (which is the worst thing I
could have said, 'cause then The Mac starts rapping
"IT'S GETTING HOT IN HERE" in front of the entire
team).

Halftime

Right after
you glance
at April waving
from the bleachers,
your stomach detonates:
KABOOM!
and you lose it
right there
behind the bench
in Pernell's gym bag.

Coach asks

Nick, you okay? Yep, better.
I need to sub you? No I'm good, Coach. *Good! Then get
in there.*

Second Half

The game's tied
when Dad finally shows up.

You throw in
to Pernell, who screens it.

Your belly's in a boxing match.
And losing. Bad.

Here comes Coby.
Pernell taunts him,

feints a pass.
Coby doesn't fall for it.

Instead he leaps like a lion,
they collide.

Pernell eats dirt,
curses.

Man against boy, Coby says.
Standing over Pernell.

The ref holds a yellow card
to a grinning Coby.

Thirty-two minutes left.
ARGGH!

Nine Minutes Left. Can't This Be Over Already?

The jabs to your belly
are almost unbearable.

Dad was right, food poisoning.
You'll never eat fish again. EVER!

Pernell's direct free kick
is wide left.

The pain is right
beneath your rib.

You dribble fast, somehow
you get in front

of Coby, and he holds you.
From behind. You slip.

The referee blows the whistle.
Play stops.

Coby gives you a hand up.
If he gets another yellow,

he's done. Game over for him.
Just a warning. Whew!

Pernell comes over, gets in Coby's face:
You think you're Messi, player, but

you're just dirty! If you wanna play
dirty, we can do that, and after

I take you down, I'm gonna make you
wash my clothes, cut

my grass, lace my cleats.
You're about to get shook, crook.

The pain only allows you to laugh
a little. Pernell is crazy, but he better

watch out, 'cause Coby, who bumps
Pernell's shoulder as he walks away,

looks pretty
freakin' pissed.

Booked

You get the ball
again and

take off
for the corner.

You almost forget
the pain. Almost.

It's sharp, like an uppercut.
There's the goal.

And there's Coby again.
Running

toward you
like a gazelle.

Your stomach can't take any more
punches.

No one in front of you
but the goalkeeper

and Coby.
You pass it to Pernell.

He shoots it
back to you.

You get ready to drive
the ball home.

Everything slo-mos
like you're in *The Matrix* . . .

And Coby is Neo.
And Neo is a bull.

And the bull's-eye is on you.
Two crazed eyes glued to the ball.

You wind for the kick. WHACK!
POW!—Coby's cleat, aiming for

the ball, finds your—THWACK!—
ankle instead. The two of you fall—WHISTLE!—

sideways, to the ground. EEE-YOW!
Your ankle POPS!

Your stomach EXPLODES!

KNOCK. OUT.

Hospital

Hello, says a woman with big ears, holding an
Otoscope in her hand. *How are you feeling?*
She asks, while looking in your eyes. Uh, I'M IN
PAIN! you scream. Dad shoots you a look.
It's okay, Mr. Hall. We're going
To find out what's going on in there.
ARRRGGGHH! IT REALLY HURTS!
Let's get the OR ready, stat, she says.

Ankle sprains

are very common
in soccer,
she says, talking fast

like she's in a hurry
to show you
the x-rays

on her iPad.
It'll heal pretty quickly,
a few days.

Cool! you think, still
in a boatload
of pain.

But I'm afraid
that's the good news.
The bad news is,

you don't have
food poisoning.
That sounds like good news to you.

You have a perforated appendix
and we need to get you
into surgery.

What does that mean? you ask.
It means that your appendix, which
is about the size of your tongue, and

located right here, she says, pointing
to the bottom of her stomach
on the right side, *has ruptured.*

There's a tear in it, and
we need to surgically
remove it

before infection sets in.
Surgery?
When?

NOW!

Surgery

I don't want to die, you say.
Everything's gonna be fine, Nick, Dad says, on the way
to the operating room.

Mom's on a flight, he adds,
so she'll be here
when you get out of surgery.

It's a quick operation, and
I've done a million of these, adds the doctor
as the orderlies roll you into the room.

195

You clench your fist, as if
that's gonna stop the ocean
of fear that's galloping toward you.

Count backwards from ten, another doctor says,
And before you completely drown,
everything goes black.

Fact

There are seventy-eight organs
in the human body
But after the appendectomy,
you have seventy-seven, which
is just about the number of
text messages
from friends
and family
awaiting you
when you wake up
in your room
a few hours
later.

How are you feeling, Nicky?

Like I just ran
a marathon,
swam a few laps,
and played back-to-back
soccer matches,
is how you answer
Mom's question.

And your stomach? Dad adds.
Like butter.
Huh?
Smooth and easy.
Smooth.
And easy, you say, giggling,
then dozing
back off
to sleep.

Bad

Your white blood cell count is elevated, the doctor says.
What does that even mean? you ask, grimacing.

Your count should be no higher than five thousand.
What is it? Dad asks, holding Mom.

*It's twenty thousand. So he'll need antibiotics to fight off
any infections.*
How long do I have to be here?

*We will just need to keep you for a few extra days, but by
then the wound should be all healed and we'll send you on
your way. Sound good?*
As long as it's only a few days, you say. I'm playing in a
big soccer tournament next week.

The doctor, Mom, Dad, even the nurse who's changing
your bandage, get all silent and stare at each other. Then
at you.

Crickets.

Worse

He'll be out of school
for a week,
or two,
depending on how he feels, the doctor says to Mom,
who rests her hand
on your heart,
which breaks into
a thousand little pieces
when the doctor adds,
You'll be back
playing soccer
in no time, Nicholas.

199

The Dallas Cup
is next week, you tell her. How long
is no time?

Only three weeks.

Only

ONLY. Three. Weeks.
but Dallas is in one.

ONLY your stomach is shattered
and your dream's undone.

ONLY not playing soccer
makes the pain seem severe.

ONLY your eyes can't conceal
tear after tear.

ONLY your ship is sinking
and you'll miss all the fun.

ONLY. Three. Weeks.
but Dallas is in one.

The End

when a horse breaks
its leg,
the bone shatters
the nerves, the living tissue
can't heal
'cause there's not
enough blood supply.
There is no recovery
from that type of
damage.

It's over.
they may as well
put you down.

TV Therapy

Mercy General has six
ESPN channels, but
this does not impress your dad.

This Sucks

Tottenham is playing Arsenal but you switch to
Hawaii Five-O, 'cause watching *fútbol* will only
Irritate you, remind you of what you're missing. Room
Service brings you cold soup, and just before
Steve's mother's murderer is revealed, Dad turns it off.
Uncool, Dad, you say. *You're not going to binge on
Cop shows or ESPN all day,* he says. Dad, the boredom is
Killing me. *Maybe you should read,* he adds, and
Slides his dictionary closer to you.

203

New Rules

You get five TV minutes
for each page read. Does it have
to be *your* book? *It does not.*

Mom kisses you goodbye

Sleep tight, Nicky, she says, and
they both walk out.
He stops
at the door, turns around,
like he forgot something,
and just stares
at you.

Books are fun, Nicholas, he says,
they're like
amusement parks
for readers.

Yeah, well, maybe
they would be fun
if I got to pick
the rides
sometimes, you answer, your eyes

glued to
the **W**s.

The Next Morning

The nurse asks if she can get
you anything. Bacon, eggs,
and french fries, please, you reply.

Breakfast

Thirty minutes later, she
returns with buttered wheat toast,
cherry yogurt, and Coby.

Conversation with Coby

Hey, Nick. What's up?
The sky.

I saw your mom and dad in the lobby.
Yeah, they never leave. It's annoying.

I think they were arguing.
Why you say that?

'Cause your mom wasn't talking, and your dad didn't look happy.
He never looks happy.

True. I was gonna come earlier, but my mom said you needed your rest.
What I need is some real food.

True.
Pernell's an idiot. I shoulda done something.

. . .

. . .

Sorry about that tackle. I was going for the ball.
Yeah, I know. I woulda scored. We woulda won.

I don't think so.
You got booked?

Yeah, ref threw me out.
Sorry about that.

How's the stomach?
It's feeling better. The food's disgusting.

That sucks.
Yeah . . . How'd you get here?

My dad.
Really?

Yeah, he's coming to the Dallas Cup.
. . .

Sorry you can't come, Nick.
Good luck.

I'll bring you something back.
Bring me a jersey or a ball.

I'll get my dad to buy us some swag. Definitely.
Coby, you miss him a lot?

Not really. We talk all the time, and I see him every summer.

Oh.

I know it's kinda hard right now, but you'll get used to it.

. . .

Hey, Man U is playing Arsenal. Let's watch.

Can't.

Huh?

Can't watch TV, uh, right now.

Dear Skip

Mac

You can find me here—

I'm

imprisoned,

trapped

by a *verbomaniac*

and locked

far

from fun,

from freedom.

Will you

PLEASE bust me out?

Save me from

this madhouse of

Boredom and

Weird Words.

Bring a decent book

ASAP.

PS. Please make it a thin book with a lot of white space on the page. Thanks!

Rapprochement*

In the middle of Scrabble
the nurse comes in
to take your
blood pressure
for the third time
today.

Out of nowhere
Mom starts crying
and apologizing
for breaking up
the family
to chase
her equine dreams.
Then Dad starts
telling her
it's not her fault
and now
he's sorry
for not paying
enough attention
to her

213

----

* **rapprochement** [rap-rohsh-mahn] *a reestablishment of harmonious relations.*
Are they getting back together?

and respecting
her career.

And then they hug
for like fifteen minutes.

Visitors' Day

While you're figuring out
the math of it all:

> (Two more days in the hospital.
> Probably watch 8 to 10 hours of TV a day.
> For a total of 1,000 to 1,200 minutes.
> Which means you have to read
> at least 200 pages.
> ARGGH!)

Guess who strolls in?

Hello, Nicholas

Ms. Hardwick?
This isn't a pigment of your imagination?

A malapropism, I remember.
Very good. How are you feeling?

I'm cured, I guess, but I can't play soccer.
I'm sorry to hear that. I didn't have appendicitis, but I had
kidney stones. It's worse. Not fun. Not fun at all.

. . .
We miss you in class.

Who is *we*?
Since you're gonna be out for a few weeks, I thought I'd
bring an assignment.

. . . (Yay me!)
Mr. MacDonald said you asked for a book, and it just so
happens, we recently started a new one.

The Mac is a traitor, you think.
He couldn't make it today, but he will stop by tomorrow,
she says, handing you a book called *All the Broken Pieces.*
I think you may find a good read here, Nicholas.

Thank you, Ms. Hardwick. I'm taking a lot of antibiotic medication, you know, so I fall asleep a lot, so I'm not sure how long it will take me to read this, you say, yawning loud so she can hear you.

Always the comedian. Nicholas, I brought someone to see you. Are you up to another visitor, or are you too sleepy? she says, with a smirk.

You glance out of the window, wondering who it is. It's probably Mr. Mac, trying to make an entrance. Sure, you answer.

Well, then, you have a grand day, and a speedy recovery. I miss my wordsmith, she says, winking.

You open the book, notice the number of pages, 240. Well, that's promising, you think, as your next guest saunters into the hospital room.

Hey, Nick.

This has got to be a *sweven*.

Got. To. Be. A. *Sweven*.
There is no way this is happening.
You must be daydreaming again.
No freakin' way.

Hi, Nick.
Uh, hi, I'm, um, April, sorry, I'm just a little stup-id. I
mean—

(And, of course, you mean *stupefied*,* but you're too
stupefied to actually say it.)

Sorry about your appendix. The whole class signed this.
She hands you a get-well card signed by everybody.

*I'm sorry you can't play soccer. That must make you feel
pretty, uh, irascent.*
You shoot her a look of surprise.

What?! It means angry.
I know what it means.

----
* **stupefy** [stoo-puh-fiy] *verb: to stun or overwhelm with amazement.* I sure
hope this isn't a *sweven*.

I've been reading your dad's dictionary, she says, smiling.
Where'd you get that?

Mr. Mac showed it to us at book club. A lot of cool words.
Wow! That's, uh, interesting. I wouldn't say it's *cool*,
though.

What letter are you on?
X.

Wow, almost finished.
I've been reading it for, like, three years.

Whoa! Tell me an X word.   219
Xu.

Sounds like a Z.
Yeah, most of the *X* words are pronounced like that.

What does it mean?
It's the money they used in Vietnam, before the war.

Like a dollar, only a xu, she says, and you stare at her lips
way too long.
Exactly.

Well, I see Ms. Hardwick gave you the Broken Pieces
book. It's really good.
You read it?

*Yep, and, get this: the boy in the book is really good at base-
ball, and he's from Vietnam. You'll like it, trust me.*
(Did she just say *get this*?)

*Okay, well, I gotta go. Text me, let me know what you
think of the book.*
Uh, okay.

*Bye, Nick. Get well soon, 'cause you and I have some danc-
ing to do,* and she kisses you goodbye on the forehead
more like a grandmother would, but that's not going to
stop you from never washing your head. Ever.

You're not really into baseball

but you give the book a chance
for obvious reasons, plus
you need to earn some minutes.

221

All the Broken Pieces

is about war
but told
by a boy
your age
who can't seem
to find peace
after a bomb
blows
his village
and his brother
to pieces.
Then a soldier
takes him
to America
where he's adopted and
just about to find out
if he's made
the baseball team
on page 54
which means
you have amassed

four hours
and thirty minutes
of nonstop
TV.

Click.

The Next Day

After a night
of channel surfing
and back-to-back
reruns
of *Star Trek,*
the morning sun
rushes in
courtesy of the nurse
raising the blinds.

You eat gooey
fruit cocktail
and just before
you power up
your tablet,
The Mac
strolls in
with his bowling bag,
and duffel,
sporting a blue and white hoodie
that reads
putyour**FACE**ina**BOOK.**

Conversation with The Mac

I brought you a gift, he says, handing
you a box wrapped in gift paper.
The dragonfly box?

Well, it is a box, he says,
plopping himself down
in the chair.

Thanks, Mr. Mac, you say, opening
the greasy, white cardboard box.
Mr. Mac, this is *KFC!*

*Yep, sure is. Bought you
a three-piece
chicken meal and a biscuit,* he says.

Uh, thanks, but I can't really eat
that kind of stuff yet, Mr. Mac.
Good, 'cause there's only

*one piece left. Give it here.
I don't know if I'm more hungry
or tired, Nick.*

. . .

I just walked from the bowling alley.
And, it was a terrible walk, 'cause I lost.

Why didn't you drive?
Lucky finally died. Had it for thirteen years.
Guess your luck ran out, Mr. Mac.

If I wasn't so tired, I'd laugh at that.
Did you get the book?
Yep, I'm reading it.

What page are you on?
Fifty-four.
Nice! Any thoughts?

Yeah, it's all poetry.
And?
It's okay.

So why're you reading it, if it's just okay?
. . .
You're reading it because April Farrow

told you to read it, he says, and
laughs so loud,
the person in the room

behind you bangs on the wall.
So what do you think
of the main character, Matt Pin?

I kinda feel bad for him,
getting picked on — I can relate.
Getting picked on by whom? The Mac interrupts.

His classmates.
They call him names
like *Frogface*

and *Matt-the-Rat* and
Rice-Paddy and —
Odd names to call someone, dontcha think, Nick?

He's from Vietnam,
so the kids treat him different.
They're prejudiced, I guess.

Can't wait to find out what he does,
'cause right now he just does nothing.
What would you do, Nick?

I'd probably stand up for myself.
And then The Mac stops talking and

drifts off, staring out your window

and you're left
wide awake, thinking of
all your broken pieces.

Read Aloud

When he wakes up
ten minutes later
The Mac
whips out
his copy,
plops down
in the vinyl chair
at the foot
of your bed,
kicks off
his white high-tops,
props both legs up,
yawns louder
than an elephant seal,
stretches,
then proceeds
to read
to you
like you're in kindergarten
and it's story time.

He sounds

like he's on the mike,
rapping.
His flow is sick.

He pops his shoulders.
Bobs his head.
All while reading.

You listen.
You laugh.
You follow along.

Didn't think
you were gonna
like this

book.
Two hours later,
when The Mac lands

on the final page,
the doctors and nurses
who've lingered

and listened, and who
crowd your room,
give The Mac

a standing ovation.

Texts to April

Hey April,
I finished
the book.

The beginning
was a little slow
but the ending was

tight.
The poems
were cool.

The best ones were
like bombs,
and when all the right words

came together
it was like an explosion.
So good, I

didn't want it to end.
I give it
an 8.6.

Sorry

For the long text.

Hey, what are you reading next?

Text from April

*I'm glad you get to go home
tomorrow, Nicky. Sending
you a pic of our next book.*

Discharged

It's 9:30 a.m.
Checkout day.
You've been up
for four hours
'cause you couldn't sleep
after thinking about
April and
the baseball book,
so you read it again,
but not the whole thing,
just the parts
you dreamed about,
and then the sun
came out,
and the remote
needed a new battery
and you were bored,
so you picked up,
            get this,
his dictionary
and you were finishing
the *Y*s, when
in walked Mom
and Dad.

Driving Home

Shotgun, you yell.
How much TV did you watch? Mom says
from the back seat.

A lot. Read a book, too.
Really?
Yep.

And you liked it?
Uh, yeah, you say. Can we
stop by the library?

I need to get another one.
Sure, and after lunch I can beat you
in Ping-Pong, Mom answers.

Naw. I mean no, I'm gonna
just chill out in my room.
I'm a little tired, you lie.

Out of the Dust

is a story
about a lanky
piano-playing girl
named Billie Jo
whose mother
is gone,
whose father's heart
and soul
are disappearing
into the dust
that blankets
their Oklahoma town,
and even though
the first 59 pages
rain down
hard on you,
when you get
to page 60
the monsoon comes
and the book is
unputdownable.

You dial April's number

six times, but each
time you hang up
before it rings
because you're nervous
and don't know
what to say,
so before
the seventh time
you decide to write down
a list of everything
you want to say
to her,
but you don't plan
on her father
answering.

238

Phone Conversation

Uh, hello, Mr. Farrow, is uh, April available?
Who is this calling?

It's me, sir, Nicholas, her friend from school.
Her friend from school. I've never met you.

Uh.
Well, what do you want, son?

I'd like to speak to her, please, sir.
About what?

About a, uh, a book that we're reading.
Oh, really, and what book would that be, Nicholas?

It's called, um . . . It's called *Dust,* um, it's—
Dad, give me the phone. Stop, you hear April scream in
the background.

*Well, Nicholas, you have ten minutes to speak to my
daughter about this book that you're reading, you understand?*
Yes sir.

Hi, Nick, my dad can be so lame sometimes, she whispers.
It's okay.

What are you doing?
I have just completed *Out of the Dust,* you answer, reading from your notes.

Sweet! What did you think?
It was stellar, and I was quite moved by its contemplation of the human spirit.

Why are you talking like that, Nick?
Like what?

You sound like a robot?
I am very much looking forward to the next book we are reading.

Stop acting silly, Nick.
. . .

I was thinking that you could pick the next book, Nick.
Me?

Yeah. The book club needs to mix it up a little.
But, uh, I'm not in the book club.

Well, you kinda are now, Nicky.
Okay, you say, laughing a little.

I'm serious, you're official now.
No, it's not that. My mom calls me Nicky.

Oh, I'm sorry.
No, you can call me that.

Okay. How is your mom doing?
She's fine.

She's still here?
Yeah, I think she's gonna stay.

241

Very cool!
. . .

So, you're gonna pick a book.
Yeah, I guess.

Maybe we can discuss the book at your house or something.
Uh, I don't know about that. My parents probably won't
let me do th—

Maybe you could ask your mom, Nicky?
. . .

So what are you doing now?

I am presently folding my clothes and preparing to clean up my room.

Oh, Nicky, you're cray-cray.

. . .

Books You Find on Google

Dear Know it All **Percy Jackson**

If You're Reading This, It's TOO LATE!

Planet Middle School

May B.

CATCHING FIRE!

BECAUSE. OF. WINN-DIXIE.

SMILE,

I Will Save You
When You Reach Me

Where the Sidewalk Ends

Until We Meet Again,

Peace, *LOCOMOTION,* *Darius and Twig:*
The Outsiders

P.S. Be Eleven

Dreams Come True

Ms. Hardwick's moving
to another state to teach

The twins got kicked out
for the rest of the year

April's coming to your house
Your family is back together

And you start back soccer soon.
Finally, normal seems possible

again.

Today, Coby called

when he got back from Dallas.
Asked you to come over.

You said no, told him
you had to clean up,

which was half true.
You didn't *have* to,

you *wanted* to,
'cause Mom said

the only way she'd let April
come over

was if you cleaned
the refrigerator,

your bathroom,
and your room,

and organized the closet.
So you limped around

and did just that
happily.

Knock Knock

Your mother answers the door,
and you hear April's voice, but
wait: she is not alone. ARGGGH!

Twain*

Thanks for inviting us, Nick, April says.
US?
Mom shoots you a look like you knew all these people
were coming.
You didn't!

Saida and Maisha
are behind April,
followed by
Annie, Kellie,
and,

        get this,
Winnifred.

---

* **twain** [twayn] *adjective: two.* This dance was supposed to be a two-step, not
a freakin' flash mob.

Nerds and Words

I can't even imagine living in a dust storm, says Kellie. *I
really felt like I was right there with Billie Jo.*
Yeah, me too, says Saida, *'cause my dad is sad a lot too.*
He's sad because he lost his job, Saida, Maisha says to her
sister, and then we're all quiet, 'cause that *is* sad.

*Well, I like that Mad Dog likes her,
but why doesn't he just tell her?* Annie says.
You mean like you wish Robbie Howard would tell you?
Kellie giggles.

And that's when you realize you're in a book club
with all girls, which is insane.
April smiles at you. *What do you think, Nick?* she asks.

Just then, your mom comes out
of the kitchen
with a tray of cookies,

and,
           get this,
tea, and

now you're sipping tea

with a bunch of girls, and
so glad

that no guys
are here
to see you.

What were you about to say, Nick?
Uh, I was just gonna, uh, say
that I liked it, I guess.

Did you have a favorite part? she asks.
You know your mom's listening
from the kitchen when you say, Yeah,

on page 205
when Billie Jo
tells her dad,

I can't be my own mother . . .

A Long Walk to Water

At the end of the meeting
Winnifred starts
blabbering

about some book
we *MUST READ NEXT*
because

her older sister says
it's hauntingly beautiful
and gut-wrenching

and it's based
on a true story
about boy soldiers

in Sudan
and she gave it
five stars

and *blah blah blah*
and April interrupts with:
I think Nicky has a suggestion.

Your Suggestion

Can we please choose
a book with a boy this time—
Weren't you listening? Winey interrupts. *It is about*
a boy.

Preferably in this time period, you continue.
I need a break from history, I'm just sayin'.
Like what? Winnifred whines.

Like *Peace, Locomotion,*
an epistolary novel, which
means a—

I KNOW WHAT EPISTOLARY MEANS, she shouts,
still frowning. *IT'S A BOOK WRITTEN IN LETTERS.*
Great choice, April says, and winks

at you.

Bye, Nick

Thanks for hosting the club, she
says, and hugs you. *Tell your mom
I can't wait for tomorrow.*

Huh?

Family Meeting

Why'd you go and do that?
I thought you'd like it, Nicky. It'll be fun.

What if I need my crutches? My ankle's still a little sore.
You'll be on a horse—why do you need crutches?

MOM, IT'S NOT FAIR. You can't just be setting up a
date for me.
It's not a date. It's just me, you, and April riding horses.

. . .

Well, I like her. She's a nice girl.

Yeah, I know.
I was thinking that for the wedding, we would—

Stop making fun!
What's all the commotion? Dad says, coming in through
the garage.

Well, your eighth grade son is afraid of a girl.
I'm not afraid, Dad. She's just setting up outings and
whatnot without my permission.

I'm afraid this is grounds for a family meeting. Meet me in the living room.
We're already in the living room, Dad.

Right! Okay, well, present your case.
You start talking and Dad interrupts—

Ladies first, sir.
Thank you, Mom says, all prim and proper-like. *Well, I met his girlfriend—*

She's not my girlfriend. I object.
So noted, says Dad. *Carry on, Milady.*

I figured he might want to hang with her outside of school, and I thought since he's so good at riding—
Nicholas, are you good at riding?

Dad, this isn't about—
Just answer the question, please.

Yes.
Do you like this April girl?

Uh, I guess.
Yes or no answer, please.

Yeah.
Will you have fun with her?

Probably, but I'm not fully recovered, and—
Are you going back to school next week?

Yes.
Based on the evidence that's been presented, I rule in favor
of the defendant. The date shall commence tomorrow.

WOOHOO! Mom yells.
That's not fair, you say.

The judge has decided, Mom counters.
Let's hug it out, Dad says,

and the three of you do,
just like old times

and hopefully new ones, too.

Text to Coby

Who beat y'all?
A team from Mexico. They were fast!

Bummer.
Your team got beat too.

I heard.
But it was cool. I met Pelé.

NO FREAKIN' WAY! REALLY?

Well, I saw him from, like, a distance, but yeah.

Cool!
So what's up with you?

Everything's great. My mom and dad are back together.
Really?

Really.
That's what's up.

Looks like you had a lot of fun in Dallas. I saw your pics.
Not as fun as it coulda been. Wasn't the same.

Same as what?

Same as if you were there. If you want, we can play FIFA after school.

Can't. I'm booked.

You're booked?

Yup. I got a date tomorrow.

A date? With who?

April Farrow.

Yeah, right. Where y'all going?

Riding horses.

Atta-boy!

257

When April

gets out
of Mom's rental SUV
and walks over
to the stable,
only one word
can describe
the way she
moves
in those
blue jeans:

*callipygous.**

---

* **callipygous** [kal-*uh*-pij-ee-gus] *adjective: having a beautiful backside.* A nice rumpelstiltskin. LOL!

Rock Horse Ranch

Use the steel comb
like this, you say to April,
demonstrate how
to remove
the caked-on dirt.

Then take this soft brush
and rub over her, yep,
just like that, to wash away
the dust.
You're doing great, April.

You know a lot about horses, Nick, she says.
I guess.
You know a lot about everything. Is it true you skipped a grade?
Yeah, second.
You're so smart, Nicky.
. . .

Okay, check her feet
with a hoof pick, to clear out
the little rocks and stuff, you say.

Are you feeling better, Nick?
Yeah, pretty much.
Are you still gonna play soccer?
Uh, YEAH!
Well, that's good. 'Cause you're pretty good.
I know.

      (We both laugh.)

Miss Quattlebaum told me
to tell you hi.
Maybe I'll be in class
on Monday, *Milady,* you say, not
looking up, and wishing
you hadn't said that.

Let's mount this pony, she says.
Whoa, cowgirl, you tell her. We
still have to put the saddle on.
Oh, right. Sorry, Nick.

Let me do the saddle, it's kind of heavy.
Want me to help you, Nick?
I'm good.
But you're not, 'cause you stumble,
fall flat
on your *rumpelstiltskin.*

Having trouble over there? Mom hollers, laughing.

Now April's trying not to laugh. And failing.

Even the horse got jokes. He neighs.

Let me help you up, cowboy, April says, grinning.

You okay?

I'm good.

You said that before, Mom hollers. Still laughing.

You jump up, saddle the horse.

Yep, let me help you up.

Mom comes over with her horse.

I've got an idea, Nicky, she says. *It's her first time, so
one of us needs to pull
April's horse around
until she gets the feel for it.*

261

I thought you were going to do it, Mom?

Uh, no, Momma's gonna be riding.

Well, I can't do it.

I'm riding too.

I'll be fine, Mrs. Hall, April says.

Mom shoots you a look.

Here's my idea, she says.

*How about for the first few times
around the field,
April rides with you.
Solves all our problems, right?*

Sounds like a plan to me, April says.

Blackjack.

Afterward

PLEASE, MOM!
We just want to
go to the mall.
It's not that late.
Her parents said
she could go.
We're just gonna
walk around,
maybe see
a movie.
Her friend
Charlene can meet us
there too.
You can come also.

THANK YOU! THANK YOU!

By the way, would you mind
sitting a few rows in front of us,
like maybe, uh, twenty-one?

You absolutely love

it each time
a zombie
lunges at a human
and chomps on flesh
because it makes April
grab the legs
next to hers,
one of which
is yours.

Thank You

I had a great time with you
and your mom. Your parents rock!
You're so lucky. Guess I am.

Later, at Dinner

Mom and Dad stop whispering
when you get to the table.
Nicky, I made your favorite, she says. *Lobster
mac-and-cheese. Figured you needed
a break from the mustard.* We both kinda laugh.
And I even made cupcakes. Red velvet, Dad adds.
By made, *your father means he MADE
his way to the cupcakery and bought them.*
We all laugh, and it feels
like love is back,
like home again,
just like it's supposed
to feel.

Conversation with Mom and Dad

Nicky?
Yep, Mom?

I'm leaving on Thursday.
What do you mean?

I've got to get back to work, honey.
But you're coming back, right?

To visit.
Huh? I don't understand.

The Derby's coming up. It's my obligation to get Bite My Dust prepared. You understand, right, Nicky? They need me.
But I thought you quit, Mom.

Quit? Why would I—
I mean, it's just that me, you, and Dad have been . . . I mean, things are normal again.

Nicholas, your mother and I have decided to get a divorce.
A DIVORCE? But, I thought, uh, I just . . . I, we—

I was afraid of this, Dad says to Mom.

Afraid of WHAT, that I would think you two would get your life together and not ruin mine again?

Your father and I love each other, and we always will, but sometimes life and work and love don't all mesh.

I don't even know what that means.

Nicholas, your mother and I are just, uh, uncompossible.

It's IN, *incompossible,** not UN. Look it up, you say, and start getting up from the table.

We're sorry, honey.

Yeah, me too. Sorry some horse's needs are more important than mine.

Nicky, come back. Let's talk about this.

. . .

---
* **incompossible** [in-kuhm-pos-uh-buhl] *adjective: incapable of coexisting, of being together.* It's official: eighth grade SUCKS!

What happens to a dream destroyed?

Does it sink
like a wrecked ship in the sea?

Or wade in the water
like a boy overboard?

Maybe it just floats
around and around . . .

or does it drown?

On the way to the airport

Mom tells you
how proud
she is
of the man
you're becoming
and makes you
promise to
call
or text her
every day,
eat healthier,
quit cutting
your nails
on the living room floor, and
keep your
grades up.

269

Maybe you and Coby want to come to the Derby, she adds.
No thanks, we have soccer obligations, you answer.

Sinking

In the car
on the way home
the engine battles
the hum of silence and
sadness
that envelops
you.

He finally says something . . . random.

Nicholas, the world is an infinite sea of endless possibility.
Yeah, well, it feels like there's big freakin' hole in my
ship, Dad.

Conversation with Dr. Fraud

Is Eminem your favorite rapper?
Huh?

The last time we spoke, you were quoting him.
He's not my favorite rapper, though.

Well, I'm more old school. Ever heard of the Fresh Prince?
The old TV show?

Yeah, but he's also a rapper.
Okay.

How did you decide to handle the bullying?
It's handled.

So it's not an issue?
I don't think so.

And what about your bike?
Uh, what about it?

Do you want it back?
Those hellkites* are gone, so that's all I really wanted.

---

* **hellkite** [hel-kiyt] *noun: an extremely cruel person.* Coby says they posted a pic of my bike and a bunch of other stuff they took from kids.

*Nice word. Your mother mentioned you were exceptionally
articulate.*
Didn't really have a choice about that.

What do you mean?
My father forces me to read his dictionary. Has since I
was nine.

What don't you like about it?
The part where I have to READ it.

Would you rather not be exceptionally articulate?
Maybe.

So you'd just prefer to be normal?
I guess.

Like everyone else?
Yep.

Even on the soccer field?
That's different.

How?
I like soccer.

And you don't like being smart?

I don't like being forced to *sound* smart.

. . .

. . .

Tell me, how do you feel about your mother leaving?
I feel like I'm drowning.

What will it take for you to get above water?
I don't know. It's outta my control. She's not coming
back, and they're getting divorced.

Can you swim?
Uh, yeah!

*So if you feel like you're drowning and you know how to
swim, then maybe you can get above water.*
That sounds crazy.

I guess it does.
. . .

How are things going in school?
School's okay, but I'm tired a lot.

Are you getting sleep at night?
I was. Probably not now.

Why not?
'Cause I'll be thinking about my mom.

How long has she been gone?
Three days, this time.

Have you spoken to her?
When she got to her, uh, new house, she called.

And since then.
Nope.

Maybe you should call or text her.

Yeah!

It's hard for her, and for you. And as hard as it is, regular communication is what gets things back to normal.
Normal? Yeah, right.

Change is hard, Nicholas, for all of us. We figure out how to cope, how to adapt, and eventually things do get back to normal.
Yeah!

. . .

. . .

*Talking about things is good. It can help you stay above
water.*

Oh, really?

Yes.

. . .

So, I'll see you next week?

Tupac.

I'm sorry?

You asked who my favorite rapper was. It's Tupac.

Keep your head up, Nicholas.   275

Yeah.

Regular Communication

Hey, Mom, I'm good, though my toe
nails have grown so long that my
hooves hurt bad. April says hi.

At Miss Quattlebaum's

The girls line up
ear to ear
so you and the other boys
can greet them
with a proper hand kiss.
Gentlemen, backs are straight and stiff, Miss Fruit
Tree says.

She passes
out gloves
to the girls,
so they
don't have to
touch
our clammy hands, you guess.

You zoom down the line, and
when you get to April,
in her blue mini-dress,
you decide
to finally
wear cool:

Uh, April, I was wondering, if you, uh, wanted to go to the eighth grade formal with me?

Regular Communication

Hey, Mom, I'm good, though I'm a
little sick of Cheetos and
grape soda. April says hi.

After School, You Stop in to See The Mac

Hey, Nick,
did you know that
outside of a dog,

a book is a man's best friend, and
inside of a dog,
it's too dark to read? he says, laughing.

C'mon, you know that was funny.
It was corny, Mr. Mac.
Before you leave, grab your flash drive

out of lost and found.
Oh, snap! Been looking for that.
It's got my outline on it.

You left it in the computer.
Dang, I sure did.
So, no soccer practice today? What's up?

Yep, I'm on the way there now, but
I wanted to give you this.
What's this?

A birthday gift.

For me? How'd you know it was my birthday?

Google.

You stalking me, Nick Hall!

You were a pretty good rapper, Mr. Mac.

Pretty good? I was dope.

You're a cool librarian. There's a surprise in the book.

Oh snap, you did another black out joint!

Yeah! Plus, I read the whole friggin' book.

How was it?

It was sad, and crazy funny, and really good, and I think you'll really like it.

Kid, you're the real deal. This means a lot.

How much?

A whole lot.

So much that you'll tell me what's inside your dragonfly box?

You want a look inside Freedom?

Huh?

My dragonfly box. I call it Freedom.

You name everything, your car, your box—
Wanna know what I call my bowling ball?
Uh, no thanks.

Fine, go ahead, open the box.
Seriously?
Go for it.

COOL!
Wait, it's locked.
Where's the key, Mr. Mac?

Ya gotta have the key
Ya gotta have the key
Ya gotta have the key if ya wanna be free.

The Mac repeats this a few times, then
takes the box back.
Real funny! Hey, Mr. Mac, why are you

so into dragonflïes?
Because they're electric, Nick.
Like bolts of lightning,

they rocket into the day.
That's how I wanna live. You?

Yeah, uh, I guess.
Well then, carry on.
I've got some work to finish.

You've got a clerk to diminish?
You know a jerk that's Finnish?
You're officially the malaprop king, Nick, he says.

Thanks again for the gift.
No problemo.

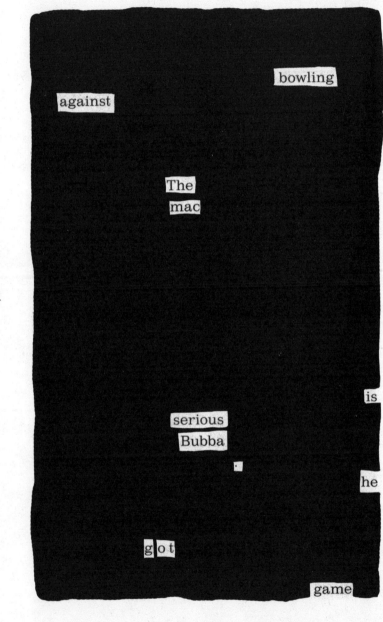

against   bowling

The
mac

is

serious
Bubba

he

got

game

Playoffs

April comes over
to wish you luck
before your first game back.

Score one for me, she says.
You don't.
You score

Two.

Text from Mom

Nicky, didn't hear from you
this weekend. How was the game?
Your texts are funny. Miss ya!

Regular Communication

Hey, Mom, I'm good. Can't talk, as
I'm in school, failing gravely.
Who cares about grades? We won!

Winnifred may be a gadfly*

but her slideshow tribute to
Ms. Hardwick is pretty swell
and it sends us all to sob town.

288

---
* **gadfly** [gad-fly] *noun: an annoying person.* In the dictionary, there's a pic of
Winnifred next to this word.

Waiting at the Bus Stop
When a Police Car Pulls Up

Hey, Nick, we can take you home.
No thanks, we're good, April.

Get in here, fellas, looks like it's about to rain.
Uh, okay, Coby says, climbing into the back seat.

Dad, this is Nick, remember?
Oh, yeah, I remember, from the phone, right? He shoots
you a look through the rearview mirror.

And this is his best friend, Coby.
Cool ride, Mr. Farrow.

Don't get used to it, son.
No sir.

I understand you play soccer?
Yes sir, we do, you say.

Who's better?
I am, sir, Coby says, all polite,

Nicholas, how is school?
It's fine, sir.

Y'all stop calling me sir. Officer is fine!

DAAAADDDDD, stop!

*April tells me you're a wordsmith or something. You a
wordsmith, Nicholas?*

Uh, I guess . . . Officer.

Are you or aren't you, son?

*DAAAADDDDD, why are you interrogating him? Leave
him alone.*

I know a lot of words, if that's what you're asking.

He sure does, April brags. *Nick, tell him about that word*
limerence.

Yeah, Nicholas, tell me about that word limerence, *the one
that my daughter has written on every notebook, plastered
all over her door, and which she now wants to tattoo on the
back of her neck. Tell. Me. About. That. Word.*

DAAAAAAAAD, STOP IT!

This is so cool, Officer, Coby blurts out.

Uh, why is the siren on?

Thirty Minutes Later

My dad's just trying to scare you.
Well, it worked.

You coming to Charlene's pool party?
I don't know.

Well, I think you should.
Okay, maybe.

Try again, Nicky.
Yeah, I guess.

Better. Text me later.
Okay. Thanks for the ride.

I can't kiss you on the cheek, 'cause my dad is look—
GOODBYE, NICHOLAS, her dad screams from the car,
then turns on the siren. Again.

Geesh, I gotta go, Nicky.
Uh, uh . . . Bye. Thanks.

I've been thinking

maybe you take
a break from
my dictionary, son.

The irony
of this
is colossal.

You laugh long
and loud like
a Guinea baboon

being tickled.
And so does he
when you say:

Well that's just perfect, Dad, 'cause
I finished it
last night.

Really? Well, that's great.
We should celebrate.
You hungry?

Very.
I'll make dinner.
How about NO, Dad.

Let's go out.
Great. I got
the perfect place.

No white tablecloths, Dad.
I was thinking
a sports restaurant.

Unlimited Hot Wings
and Soccer.
YEAH!

Conversation with Dad

Your dad
is always full
of words
to hurl at you,
but tonight,
for once,
he's wordbound.*

So are you.

. . .

. . .

These wings are good.
Yeah.

. . .

. . .

Dad, can I ask you a question?
Of course.

Did you ever get into a fight at school?

----
* **wordbound** [wurd-bound] *adjective: unable to find expression in words.*
Kinda ironic, right?

Fights? No.

. . .

Not at . . . school.

. . .

There was this kid at church named Skinny who picked on me.

Really?
He sat behind me in Sunday school and would slap me on the neck. We'd be at the fountain, and he'd spit water on me. One time when it was raining, he even tripped me and I busted my lip. It was Easter and I was wearing a brand-new white suit.

Oh, snap! What did you do?
I ran to my mom, bleeding and crying.

Oh.
But my dad came over and dragged me to the bathroom.

What'd he do, fuss at you?
No, he cleaned me up, and asked me a question.

What?
What would you do if you weren't afraid?

That's what he asked you?
Yep, and I told him, Maybe fight him.

What'd he say?
"Bullies don't like to fight, son. They like to win. Being afraid is normal. The only fight you really have to win is the one against the fear."

What does that even mean?
And then he said, "You got this" and walked out.

What'd you do?
I cried some more, then went back outside, where all the kids were, and walked right up to Skinny, and said, "Hey, Skinny, I'm sick of your yobbery.*" And then I put up my dukes.

You, uh, put up your *dukes*, Dad?
Yeah, I was ready to fight, Nick! I dodged and weaved like Muhammad Ali. He looked a little confused, maybe even a little afraid. I charged him like a bull, knocked him to the ground.

That's so cool, Dad. What happened next?
He got up and punched me in the eye. I had a black eye for two weeks.

----
* **yobbery** [yob-uh-ree] *noun: hooliganism.* He's still weird, but my dad's got a little swag.

Dang! Sorry, Dad.

Don't be. Your granddad was right. Skinny stopped mess-ing with me after that. I mean, he used to make jokes about me, but even that stopped after a while.

That really happen, Dad?

Sure did.

Should we get some more wings, Dad?

Should we knit some floor swings?

It's gotta make sense, Dad.

Should we quit before Spring?

Well done, Dad.

Good, now let's order more wings.

Hey, Mom

Dad's at a conference. I'm
home alone. It's house party
time! YEAH! Holla! Giddy-up!

Mom Calls Immediately

He's just gone for the day. I'm fine, you tell her.
After she finishes worrying, you ask her
how to make Dutch pancakes,

but it sounds too complicated,
so you stick to
instant oatmeal.

After breakfast
and a quick game
of FIFA online

with Coby,
you shower,
grab your gear,

and head out
for the match
when you hear

Morning, Nick!

Blue Moon River

Standing outside
leaning against
a light blue convertible car
is The Mac.

Hey, Mr. Mac. What's up?
You forgot this. Again, he says, handing
you your flash drive
with Hardwick's almost finished
persuasive essay on it.

Thanks. You rock, Mr. Mac!
Maybe you need to wear it
around your neck.
That's your new car?

Blue Moon River.
Huh?
It's a 1972 Ford Mercury Brougham Montego drop-top.
Pretty zazzy!*

Interesting name for a car, though.

----
* **zazzy** [zaz-ee] *adjective: stylish or flashy.*

Nicholas, there's only a hundred or so of these left.

Oh, I get it—it's rare, like *once in a blue moon.*

Exactly! Me and Blue Moon River are searching for the rainbow's end.

Uh . . . okay, but why River?

Nick, the river is always turning and bending. You never know where it's going to go and where you'll wind up. Follow the bend.

That's pretty deep, Mr. Mac.

Stay on your own path. Don't let anyone deter you. Eartha Kitt said that.

Who's Bertha Schmidt?

Nicholas, turns out Ms. Hardwick isn't the only one leaving, he says.

What do you mean?

Langston Hughes will be looking for a new librarian, too.

You're not coming back?

I'm not coming back.

Why?

Because the river turns, and there's a lot of world to see.

Are you following Ms. Hardwick?

You're a smart kid.

A new book for you,
he says, reaching
into the bag
on the ground next to him.

Thanks. *Rhyme Schemer*'s a dope title, Mr. Mac.
Is this your autobiography?
It's not, but you're gonna dig it.
The question is will it rip my heart out
and stomp on it?

I'm outta here, he says, jumping
into Blue Moon River.
Don't forget your bag, you say,
picking it up to hand to him, but

right before he speeds off
The Mac yells,
That's yours too. Be cool, Nick.

Inside the Bag Is, Get This, FREEDOM

You unlock
The Mac's dragonfly box
fully expecting
bursts
of electricity
to flitter
and flutter
like blue lightning
like souls
on fire.

What you see
is even better.
WHOA!

Sub

Coach finally puts you in.
It feels good to run toward
something, and not away . . .

After the Game

At Charlene's pool party you
see Coby, April in a
pink swimsuit, and, uh, your bike.

While you and Coby

play blackjack,
you notice
The Twins

taunting some poor kid, jabbing
the air
with their red boxing gloves.

There's a first time
for everything, you think,
and a black eye

or a bruised rib
can't hurt any more
than *appendicitis.*

I'll be right back, you tell Coby.

HEY, DEAN, you scream

He turns around.
Actually, everyone
at the party turns around.

I'm sick of your *yobbery*.
You want some of this?
Apparently he does, 'cause

he comes charging
at you
like a red bull.

As he nears, you start,
  get this,
dodging and weaving and

singing
in your best Quattlebaum voice
One-two-three, two-two-three.

When he gets to you,
you slide swiftly
to the right,

like you've got the ball
at your feet,
leaving your leg out

just enough
to trip him
face-first

into the pool.
Oh, you've really done it now, Nick.
Geesh!

One Down, One to Go

Nick? What are you doing? Coby says.
I got this, you say.
Not sure if you really do, but

realizing there's no turning back now.
Dean's doggy paddle
        (apparently he can't swim)

sends everyone
into a fit of raucous laughter.
Everyone except his brother,

who is now walking
your way,
looking murderous.

He's a few feet away
when you realize that
no dance move or soccer trick

is gonna stop his death blow.
You glance down at the table
that separates you

from his wrath.
There's a book on it:
The Heroes of Olympus.

Ironic, you think.
(Fight the fear, Nick.)
(You got this, Nick.)

Don, wait a minute. Don't you want
one more day with a chance? you ask,
quoting Michonne

from *The Walking Dead,* but
without the samurai sword.
He looks confused,

maybe even a little scared.
He kicks the table out of the way.
You want some of these paws? he says.

Do I want some **straws**? you mock.
You want my ***draws?*** **What!?**
Hey, DJ, you scream, wild and crazy-like,
DROP THAT BEAT!

And now Don looks really confused.
The crowd starts laughing, and

he throws a right punch

and you suddenly remember
how to block a punch
from tae kwon do.

It works and
you feel good,
and for once

you're above water.
And that feels great
till a left

uppercut
pops up
outta nowhere

and your jaw feels
like it is in
your brain

and wait,
who shut off
All. The. Lights.

Ouch!

You don't see stars, but, above,
you do see Charlene's mother,
Coby, and your girlfriend's smile.

Freedom

I thought you were dead.
Don't worry about me, Coby. I know how to take a punch.

Yeah, right in the face. You went down like a mattress. And then you hit your head on the table.
That hurt.

It was still kinda cool, though, the way you took Dean down.
He okay?

Yeah, he started screaming that he was drowning, then Don got him out and they left.
Cool!

Maybe they'll leave us alone now.
If they know what's best for them, they will.

What? Ballet?
Hey, it worked, didn't it?

I guess. Either that or Charlene's mother threatening to call the police worked. Oh, they left your bike, too.
Really?

Yep.
Hey, did April give me mouth-to-mouth resuscitation?

Nope, but Winnifred did.
WHAT?!

Just kidding.
She's going to the formal dance with me.

No way.
Yep.

Cool.
You should ask Charlene, then we can double date.

Yeah, maybe! Let's get outta here.
Let me say goodbye to April first. Come with me.

Seriously, dude.
Oh, I almost forgot. The Mac let me open his dragonfly box.

No freakin' way!
Yep.

Oh, snap!
You'll never believe what was inside . . .